Dedication

To Neal Cassady, here's your story

Table of Contents

Forward by; Daniel Knauf 1

Introduction 4

I stole Oppenheimer's car. 9

Initiation @ Saint John's Military School 11

Top Secret Library Duty 14

THE COMMANDANT CHEWS ME OUT 17

Private Fucko Wants to Kill a Cadet under Fire. 19

They Gave Me a Pass to Freedom 22

Chance Meeting at Col Mosby's Ditch 24

Hustling Pool in a Ghostly Dodge City Saloon 26

It wasn't the Drugs; it was the lack of them. 30

Back to Chula Vista 33

Yea fuck it, I'm stealing Oppenheimer's car. 35

The dirty deed 38

Road to the Rincon Escape from LA 42

Bre'r Trinitite Crow Blesses my Journey 44

The Country Punk Hitchhiking Cowgirl 47

The Oppenheimer Doohickey 49

PRESENT DAY HERE & NOW 1975 @ Shady Dave's 52

Fleecing the Rubes; a chump change parlor trick. 54

Back to the road to the Rincon trip. 56

SHORE PATROL LEADS MY PATH TO THE BEACH HOUSE 58

Project Morning Glory 60

Daisy Chain Old Bear Armstrong Tall Tale About Ending War 62

FREE LSD IS GROWING EVERYWHERE FOLKS 64

Keep America Beautiful 66

God Bless the Youth International Party! YIPPIE! 68

Abbie Hoffman Says; I'd Like to Buy The World A Trip 70

Yippies are good at keeping secrets secret...71

What would Doctor Oppenheimer do, challenged with providing free LSD for the people to end war? 72

Trancelike came the Gryphon..74

What next? 76

YIP Tricks Cults into Project Morning Glory; Free LSD for the People! 78

Heavenly Blues by God, by God, Heavenly Blues @Walt Disney's Grave...80

What the cult leaders didn't know 82

FREE LSD FOR THE PEOPLE; ENDING WAR FOR GOOD! 83

Playing our Secret Hometown Game...85

Chance encounter Werner von Braun 87

Walt Disney's Grave to Monte's Resort 90

We simply needed a ritual first, always a ritual of some sort. 92

Rootie Toot Toot & Yellow Security Soles 94

Drop Off @The Clean Room..97

This machine birthed what is now known as the Internet!...............99

Regardless this machine has been my part time toy about ten years. 102

I'm at The Lab. Jack Parsons Lab, JP fucking eL.........................104

JPL campus alone in the wee hours of the morning is truly a unique experience. 106

Those old paperclip Nazis were a trip, always something out of left field with them..107

Psst, It's a National Secret 108

It's rumored that Jack Parsons' death was a hoax...........................109

Voyager and the Pi tin..111

Poop in a Pi Tin..113

Yeah, that really happened. What can I say? 115

Free Sample Chapter 1 118

Forward by; Daniel Knauf

Billy Burke is exquisitely sketchy.

He's warm, funny and dangerous. I've known him since 1964, 1st grade, when he cruised the playground at St. Bede the Venerable School like Steve McQueen in THE GREAT ESCAPE, eyes scanning the yard for weaknesses in security, points of egress—anything to give him an edge should opportunity arise.

Cool and charismatic as fuck. Billy was the kind of kid who expertly worked the system, regularity committing high misdemeanors under the very noses of the Sisters of Immaculate Agony that operated the joint.

In those years we shared at St. Bede's, we ran with two different crowds so our contact was ephemeral—aware of one another, yes, but not yet friends.

We shared a lively, one night collaboration in the summer of '74, when our respective folks happened to rent cottages on Balboa Island, picking up two sweet 14 year-old locals and making out on the promenade by the neon lights of the Fun Zone until dawn (don't get your panties in a pedo-bunch—Billy and I were 16 and it was aggressively consensual on the part of the locals).

Soon thereafter, Billy got packed off to military academy and we lost touch. As for me, I decided to finish college, bear down and pursue the life of a suburban normie. There was no room in that world for rakish outlaws with switchblade smiles.

In 2008 or so, I was riding the crest of a slump. My parents had died in close order, my first marriage was in the early stages of a slow-motion train wreck and my career was faltering. I had to quickly sell the furnishings of my studio. I'd heard Burke was an auctioneer. This unpleasant occasion kindled a friendship that has lasted to this day.

Billy Burke has seen me through the best and worst moments of my life. He's been Johnny On-the-spot when all the other Johnnies were hiding out until the yellow crime-scene tape came down.

The reason I've dragged you down this sordid if colorful stretch of memory lane is to demonstrate why I don't just love Billy Burke; I trust Billy Burke.

No matter how outlandish, outrageous, absurd and impossible his narratives are, one can take them to the bank and they'll cash like precious metal—or strategic alloys, depending on the grift he's playing.

They're so true that if they aren't true, they're still true.

I Stole Oppenheimer's Car represents a chunk of those years when we lost touch after the Fun Zone. I've since heard bits of these tales over 10,000 cigarettes, gallons of good scotch and an impressive array of illicit and/or illegal substances better left unrecorded.

Had anyone else written it, I would have appreciated it as a superb post-modern gonzo take on late-70s America, resonant of Ken Kesey. But this was Billy Fucking Burke. So my first question was not, "When did you learn how to write this well?"

No. It was, "Is this shit true?"

"Most everything is," Billy drawled.

"And what isn't," I replied, "still is."

"Yup," he said.

Besides A Confederacy of Dunces, it is, hands down, the best debut novel I've ever read, its voice clear and true, mature and muscular. The telling, the same as if you were sitting across the table from The Teller.

Hate it or love it, you'll never forget it.

~ **Daniel Knauf**

Cremona, Italy

July 12, 2023

Introduction

This is a true story.

Those men in black back in Washington, DC that fateful spring of 2001 were just there as a reminder. After their visit I told myself, "They don't give a fuck about Oppenheimer's car" twenty-five years later.

Billy Burke was riding on 'top of the world, Ma', having just led the team to win the largest auction contract in the history of our blue planet. Selling the entire US Military surplus on a profit share contract using an online auction designed in the spare bedroom before our youngest son Grayson was born, April, 1999.

My online B2B auction startup was the last dot-com to be institutionally funded during the bubble, getting $13.86 million in the spring of 2000. We relocated from the Ocean City beaches to K Street, inside the beltway in Washington DC, growing a mile a minute. I was being groomed by lobbyists, admirals, Wall Street's biggest names for an IPO that would make everyone involved filthy rich.

It was a weird experience to have the sitting vice president of the United States, Al Gore, being my landlord while auctioning 'butterfly ballot voting machines'. The Supreme Court of the United States was deciding if Gore or George W. Bush would be president over some flap about 'hanging chads' in Palm Beach.

That auction was picked up by over 1,100 news media outlets in a single week, giving me and my dot-com startup a lot of exposure.

Gore 2000 had rented four floors of prime DC 'Gucci Gulch' office space near Foggy Bottom as national presidential campaign headquarters. The Vice President's daughter had to remind the second-generation politician they really were from Tennessee, not DC, relocating campaign HQ back to Chattanooga.

The presidential campaign gave my startup a full floor for half price, leaving a bunch of thrashed out furniture and office supplies mixed with empty kegs &stuff; it looked like a college dorm at semester break when we moved in.

This OG Cyberpunk, hard core punk rock serial entrepreneur had finally hit the big time. My PRE-IPO dot-com had just won a ticket to financial success with a seven-year exclusive contract with the US Military to auction everything on a profit share.

I thought they had screened and scrutinized my operation pretty thoroughly prior to being allowed as a bidder on the contract.

How can we gently say I was subjected to a proctological security clearance examination by a number of alphabet soup agencies from the accountants, military intelligence, criminal; the men in black were last to visit us.

It was a beautiful day in my offices overlooking the corner of 21st and K Streets a few blocks from the White House. I was called from my Founders office for a meeting in the conference room. Upon entry immediately noticed my "partners", Bill Angryman & Jaime Minimalist Technocracy, seated across from two "men in black" festooned in typical dress of federal agents who do security background checks.

As a NASA brat growing up near JPL, having been involved with more than one top secret project in my youth, at a glance, I knew immediately what they were and how they would operate.

I sat with my "partners" facing the two as one announced, "This is a strictly routine background clearance check; we have gone over everything submitted and just have a few questions." He spoke rather dryly, without emotion or inflection projecting a flat-line G-man.

The Man in Black started with Bill Angryman asking what his father did for a living, a few questions about associates in college, pretty much the same line of questions for Jaime Minimalist Technocracy, a French citizen already cleared by Interpol and the CIA, so they were quick with him.

Jaime was asked, "Are you now or have you ever been a member of the communist party?" To which Jaime blurted out, "Only a fool would believe Lenin's foolish teachings, following Stalin into the Abyss is for uneducated lemmings, I think not, sir, no, never." He turned away exuding an educated arrogance only the French possess and can convey.

When it came my turn the Men in Black asked, "What did your father do for a living when you were growing up?"

Taking a deep breath, scanning everyone at the boardroom table with my eyes, I replied, "He was a rocket scientist at JPL, in La Cañada." As taught, nothing more, nothing less, always the same stock answers they drilled me on as a child.

Pavlov's dog training instantly kicked in, controlling my breathing, energy, vibrations, and thoughts focused on interrogation lessons with that old kraut.

The man in black to the left asked, "Do you know what he did there, what *exactly* he worked on?" Going into well-rehearsed, piercing eyes gave this guy an 'intimidating as I can' look on his face.

Briefly pausing, I exhaled and repeated for the umpteenth time in life, always pausing and inflecting in the same spots, "Most of it was classified top secret, high security stuff, but I was in the JPL Boy Scout troop. Dad, he talked about working on Scout and Mariner, other than that he never talked about work, ever, verboten."

My mind drifted back to my parents' childhood living room filled with "retired" Operation Paperclip Nazis Dad worked with who loved Mother's lasagna and home style Italian cooking.

Non-filtered cigarettes smoldering in ashtrays, scotch & beer with never ending bar service always staple ingredients. Along with chatter about what are now called 'conspiracy theory' projects they were actively engaged in, those guys never stopped working. Something about thought leadership.

Man in Black continued his questioning without any change in posture or composure. "Were you ever on any classified, secret, or top secret project locations in the Southwest, particularly California, Nevada, and Arizona?"

I simply answered, "Yes." Bill and Jaime looked at me in astonishment.

The next question delved directly into the deepest darkest closest held secret of my life;

"What about Oppenheimer's car?" the one who had not spoken a word growled, with both of the men in black staring me down as if they had telepathic powers to read the innermost thoughts of my mind.

Cool as a cucumber, I spun Al Gore's old high backed expensive black leather presidential candidate chair around, staring back into his eyes, crisply replying, "What about it?"

With that the Men in Black closed their notebooks breaking a loud silence with a snapping sound of leather. "We are finished. Congratulations on your contract." They left the building without incident seemingly concluding their business at hand.

After the meeting my partners quizzically asked what that was about Oppenheimer's car.

I shrugged and replied, "Nothing. It's an inside joke with the JPL security people." Then I directed the conversation toward the project at hand. Nothing about that meeting was ever mentioned aloud again.

With that, as Frank Discussion, I neatly compartmentalized the memory of Oppenheimer's car back into the furthest reaches of memory, hopefully never to arise again.

Note: Memories of Oppenheimer's car have been sealed in a special compartment of my mind under sacred oath to the highest powers; that past is not in this now. It's erased or on hold until being called to remember in this now, now to deliver the message.

The men in black back in Washington DC that fateful spring of 2001 were just there as a reminder. I told myself, 'They don't give a fuck about Oppenheimer's car twenty-five years later.

Or do they?'

My reward for leading the team to win the largest auction contract in the history of our blue planet was to be terminated for cause. (That meant they wouldn't have to pay me 15% of the profits from the military contract or about $60 million in hard cash money.)

They 'legally' fired me from the company I personally founded in 1994 through an "ouster" to take most of my stock (four years prior to the IPO). The rest was taken with a gun against my head, threats of infinite dilution in 2001 at the bottom of the dot com bust. Value after the IPO peaked around $350 million that should've been paid as cash in my pockets.

Coincidence or some sort of weird karmic debt for what I, as Frank Discussion had done as a seventeen-year-old incorrigible teenager.

C'est la vie, what's a couple three hundred million dollars compared to the adventure of a lifetime.

After all, Frank Discussion had been told stealing Oppenheimer's car was in fact a very big deal, but I didn't know it at the time.

I stole Oppenheimer's car.

Outlaw Runaway Escapes 'Atomic War in Space via Military Academy'

*I*t wasn't until I got to Tijuana that I realized it was true – I stole Oppenheimer's car.

When the sun came up today I was Billy Burke, a cadet at Saint John's Military Academy being groomed for West Point. With it came nuclear war in space. Man, do I hate war. It was the Saturday after first quarter grades came out. I had scored the highest test scores in the history of the Academy, top 2/10ths of 1% in the National ASVAP equivalent of 1975. Off the charts results, me with zero fucks to give about living a militarized lifestyle.

Test scores made me a celebrity with the old Marine colonels running their precious militarized Hitler jugen (youth) academy who were as bad as Werner Von Braun and his paperclip crew at the Jack Parsons Lab I grew up with as a NASA brat.

I was smart & fast. Dean's honor roll, National Honor Society, top debate & fencing team member, tied for being the fastest runner, with the best dope in school, who saved my weekly allowance, self-funding my escape.

Forty-one cadets had attempted escape during my brief tenure; all forty-one were caught. I was imprisoned in a repository for bad boys from around the globe, all confined to experience bad ass discipline. When one escaped, a four State All Points Bulletin (APB) was put out. 41 got caught for being stupid. Not me; I'm not getting caught, no siree [sic] bub.

Penalty for getting caught attempting to escape Saint John's Military School was 444 hours marching 'perfect tours' in full dress uniform, carrying a twenty-two-pound target rifle. Every waking hour not in class or performing some demeaning act, under supervision of upperclassmen, was spent endlessly marching fifty-five feet, stopping, saluting, about face, fifty-five feet back. Lather, rinse, repeat for life of your hellish tours.

I watched them all, never once discussing my plan for escape; just watching and learning. I never marched a single tour during my captivity at Saint John's Military Academy as a rat or upperclassman.

It wasn't because I kissed ass or didn't have any attitude. It was because I was cool, had the best drugs in the Academy, and took out 'Tiny' along with four upperclassmen who tried to "initiate" me.

Initiation @ Saint John's Military School

My first day I was in my dorm room settling in when four upperclassmen rushed in, threw me on the ground, each holding an arm or a leg, talking smack about 'Tiny' building a road. 'Tiny' is an oversized Swede, blond hair, blue-eyed, 6'2" model of Aryan manhood, strong as an ox with a goofy twisted laugh saying, "I'm going to build a road on your chest."

As he twisted a wire coat hanger in his hand, I blurted out, "A road, what's a road on my chest?" Panicking in my mind but remaining completely still, I was being held down by four large cadets dressed in fatigues.

Tiny's eyes glazed with the twisted intensity of a psycho killer or a demented child who tortured small animals for sport. He twisted a flat end of that wire coat hanger, and then started making a fast, rubbing motion with it in the air, back and forth as one of the cadets holding me pulled my shirt open. "I'm going to rub a red bloody road with this right up the middle of your chest," as he leaned down into me with a look in his eyes like he was really going to enjoy hurting me.

My mind went calm like a pool of crystal-clear water as master taught me. I breathed in through my bones, twisted my legs free, leaning back using Aikido leverage of my arms being held down to balance perfectly. I pulled my legs back into my chest as far as I could, then firmly planted both of my big black brand new size 12 combat boots into Tiny's chest, with every measure of my being.

He was thrown out the door, across the hall into the wall where Tiny slumped to the floor, gasping for air as my kick knocked the wind out of his evil lungs.

Pulling my arms free in a simple circular motion I had been taught as a child, I jumped into Tiger stance, screaming something that sounded like it was from a Bruce Lee movie, "Who's next?"

As I challenged those bullies to make a move, they didn't know what to do, looking at each other, at me standing in a kung fu ready position growing, then over to Tiny, who by now was six shades of purple gasping for breath. They ran out of the room, grabbed Tiny still gasping against the wall, quickly hustling him down the hall.

Tiny came and apologized later saying it's a hazing ritual for 'Rats' or new cadets, I was the only 'Rat' or new Senior and they heard I was from California and a hippie freak.

He turned out to be a nice guy if you weren't one of his victims. Nobody ever threatened me with physical harm or bullying after that, I guess taking out the baddest motherfucker, without even thinking, made everyone else think I was some sort of bad ass.

Nope, I hate violence, but those lessons in everything included martial arts, which, if used properly, help avoid violence. Sure helped me avoid having a bloody red road built on my chest with a twisted coat hanger as a welcome to Military School initiation present.

Saint John's Military School, at the time during my 1975 tenure was something like being in a horror movie about military school institutions. RATS were degraded as less than human and everyone had to going through it, no exceptions. Hell I made it out honest after eating "squared meals" where a cadet must sit 100% upright, using fork, knife or spoon, in a squared set of motions. Dripping, was discouraged by being talked down to, actually brutally shouted at, as less than a human being, for not being able to properly "square" a complete meal.

Totally degrading one as a human being, 24-hours a day, tradition probably maintained to this day. The stories from there were pretty horrific and can be regaled another time if anyone is interested. Suffice it to say, it was living the nightmare of being sent to military school, threatened by angry parents across the nation.

Top Secret Library Duty

Saint John's Military Academy was run by a group of retired Marine Colonels, with Sergeant Titus a survivor of the Burma Death March thrown in as good measure. Everything was planned, classes like in the Corps (Ooo Rah) were based upon aptitude, ability, and security clearances were handed out like candy.

Shortly after arrival I was escorted up a metal stairway to a room with a door labeled 'Top Secret' where I had to sign a library slip of 'Top' secrecy that went into a small wooden file box in the usually empty 'librarians' desk.

There before me sat a set of books I had seen only once before @ Jack Parsons Lab Library – a complete boxed set of mission records for every rocket launched by the USA and its allies. The Holy Grail for a space geek like me, even as a child prodigy I was never granted full access to spaceflight records.

If you didn't know over 90% of America's rocket launches contain one or more 'Classified' elements, some shots aren't even on public record. Here they are, all of them. I was told, two hours daily reading anything I chose, per the Colonels' orders, instead of "regular" military school activities.

I went right for the mission index with key codes as to payload classification, type, what, when, where, results, for thousands of rocket launches. Recognizing many project names from hearing about them with my father & his cronies, plus a few I learned about rooting around in the underground cities.

In less than a week I noticed a pattern of nuclear mischief in space. Half their shit was fucked up, using wrong theorems I immediately figured were destined for failure. They had launched hundreds of nuclear reactors into space. One rocket with a nuclear reactor-based launch platform, armed with nine thermonuclear missiles, was blown up by the RSO after wobbling during takeoff, spewing radioactive materials hundreds of miles, down range.

Several nuclear bomb space station platforms were in place, with testing for manned nuclear space station components scheduled to happen in multiple launches. Diagrams, photos, trajectories, audio &video recordings, each launch had a complete file for my personal review in this top-secret library @ bumfuck Kansas.

As an assignment I was required to scribble a short one-page report of my thoughts on each mission. I just said fuck it writing notes on their 'Top Secret' DOD military forms as I read through. Scribbling my thoughts on stuff along with mathematical scratch notes, and of course, whatever I thought they were wrong about. It seemed I got as much sick pleasure out of proving militarized rocket scientists wrong, as Tiny did from building red roads on people's chests or torturing small animals.

They had a coffee pot, water dispenser, and ashtrays, meaning I could smoke away from Kansas weather that was getting colder by the day. I spent far more than my two-hour daily minimum here. It was fascinating, plus no rat abuse from upperclassmen.

Seems our US Military was gearing up for full blown nuclear war from space by 1979. Platform-based launch vehicles all banned since President Kennedy's nuclear non-proliferation treaty, which outlawed nukes in space. I was just caught up in it all because there was nothing I didn't understand, except when their theories were flawed.

Lemme tell you, nuclear war in, near, or from space is a bad idea. A really bad idea! I always thought space flight was supposed to be cool;

not being an asshole dropping thermonuclear popsicles from heaven above because Ivan likes vodka and John Fitzgerald likes scotch.

War ain't cool, killing people hand to hand like they teach @ 11:11 AM ain't cool, crisp-frying hundreds of thousands or millions of people from a single nuclear strike is totally un-cool. I just wanted to be cool, wondering why we can't just use this stuff for free energy like they promised.

Fuck management.

THE COMMANDANT CHEWS ME OUT

*O*n *a sunny brisk October afternoon, I was called into the commandant's office. Dressed in the uniform of the day, I crisply saluted an old withered up Marine colonel sitting in full uniform behind his desk, smoking a cheap, stinky cigar. "Burke, we have a letter from your father with an appointment application to West Point, signed by Senator Alan Cranston, a liberal fucking democrat from California..."*

Puffing up a big cloud of smoke, he leaned into his big desk trying to figure me out. Just what the fuck was this kid up to? "Department of Defense has taken an interest in your revelations about their space flights." Puffing a huge cloud of smoke, what looked like an Oppenheimer cloud building above his head, continuing. "Looks like they want to groom a smart ass genius for nuclear war in space."

The Colonel leaned back in his leather swivel chair looking me up and down, shaking his head. Taking another puff, he continued. "Sergeant Titus is a pretty good judge of character. He says you're a hippie freak from California with a stash of drugs. He found this hidden in your room."

Reaching into the top drawer of his desk, the Colonel held up a small bottle of patchouli oil purchased from a hippie head shop on Hollyfuckingwood Boolyvard. "Titus says you are a drug using piece of shit not fit for the Corps, Burke. Nuclear war in space isn't for druggies, Burke. Are you a piece of shit druggie or are you a cadet, Burke?"

I nervously laughed and said, "No disrespect intended, sir that is a bottle of hippie patchouli oil incense. It's used to clear one's chakras to prepare for entry into a higher plane, totally legal and certainly not some sort of illicit drugs, sir." I crisply saluted standing at attention, trying my best to hide that Burke smirk which has gotten me into more trouble than I'd care to mention.

The Colonel continued puffing away, speaking with deadpan authority. "This is going to DOD labs for testing. Nuclear war with a space cadet going to West Point, sent by a nut job liberal left-wing California Senator because daddy knows him, probably from Hollyfuckingwood."

Scowling, he stopped and stared me down for a few moments. "I know a few cadets who would like to kick the living shit out of anyone who uses drugs here at our sacred institution. They will kick the living shit out of you if, if, if this turns out, turns out to be something. Until then, innocent until proven guilty. Dismissed." We saluted; I did a precise about face, exiting his office with a sigh of relief as the door closed behind me.

The bottle of honey hash oil was tucked neatly inside the two pair of socks I wore, as it had been since my arrival. The patchouli was just bait in case somebody ran their mouth. I now knew there were real rat fink rats walking the halls and walls of this institution.

Private Fucko Wants to Kill a Cadet under Fire.

One night after smoking some of my hash oil in the NHS society lounge until 2:22 AM with four of the five top ranking cadets, I was going to sleep blissfully stoned to a faraway dreamland. About an hour or so later the Battalion Commander top ranking cadet, one of the four, entered my dorm room. He ordered me to attention, which I did sleepwalking.

In a stern military voice, he barked a series of orders to this stoned cadet. Still in a honey oil dream, I saluted with a sharp, sir yes sir, he quickly exited my room, and I jumped back into my bunk, falling dead asleep.

Next thing I remember was being awakened by our Company Commander shaking me again. I jumped out of bed, sleepwalking at attention. He barked orders; I saluted sir, yes sir. He quickly exited, then still sleepwalking, I jumped back into bed. It was like being in an opium dream, except honey hashish oil induced bliss on that god forsaken Kansas prairie.

What seemed like a few moments later my roommate Rafael des Morales, champion bowler of all Venezuela, (229 Average), who spoke little to no English, sprang out of bed and ran into the hall screaming in

Spanish at me. Then he turned and ran wearing nothing but boxer shorts and a wife beater.

Rafael was screaming like a wounded matador, with his feet on fire, running down that hall. Then hearing a big door clang shut brought me out of my stupor.

Now I was awake, remembering the other cadets' barked orders, so I swung off my bunk and walked into the hall. Looking toward the far end I could see smoke, lots of smoke, but it was a good seventy to eighty feet away in the old section of the building. Checking the nearby dorm rooms, doors open beds empty, I groan. "Fucking fire. Oh shit, everyone's gone. It's cold outside."

I went back into my dorm room, got fully dressed as ordered by the Colonel, fatigues, bloused boots, Charlie Jacket had a pack of Camel filters in the zippered sleeve pocket, and the smoking lamp was obviously lit. Grabbing a cup of coffee from a half full, simmering pot in the hall, I sauntered into that cold Kansas night toward the assembly area in my perfect uniform, puffing away to witness the entire battalion of students lined up in various stages of dress.

Most cadets were freezing in pajamas, a few had robes on, and there was ice on the ground as I looked over at fire trucks screaming into the main parade grounds. A quarter of the main school / dorm building was engulfed in flames at the far end, away from my room.

I got chewed out for being last by the senior cadet who first woke me up for being fully dressed until I repeated my direct orders from the commandant to be in full uniform of the day, at all times. "Sir, an order is an order. Sir, take it up with the commandant." Saluting Herr Student lead Kapo whilst sporting the Burke smirk.

His baked on my hash oil response was, "Burke, get in line."

I sauntered to my squad spot, Camel filter in hand, and stood with a shivering Corps of Cadets, waiting for the next order to be given.

Most other cadets just looked at me like who the fuck is this guy, last one out, warm in full uniform, smoking, drinking a coffee, probably high on something, just checking things out like the fire is a TV show or tonight's entertainment?

Well, it wasn't my style of entertainment, that's for sure.

It turned out one of the students was a killer, who enjoyed his arson killings. He had set a light bulb bomb to explode at 3:33 AM in hopes of killing a few cadets. Cadet Private Fucko was a sick motherfucker from Vermont who later in life turned into a serial killer, another story. Nobody was ever caught; I just heard who it was via the rat line scuttlebutt drumbeat.

Hearing that fire was murderous arson was all I needed to put my simple plan into action, without telling a soul, not a soul. I couldn't trust a single one of these rat fink scum sucking sum-bitches.

Being on the Dean's Honor Roll combined with my off the chart test scores instantly made me an upperclassman; it was my senior year after all. The colonel had commandant of cadets tell me I was cleared, it was hippie oil, not to ever bring anything like that on campus again.

Upperclassmen got Saturday passes into town, unsupervised in your civilian clothes passes.

One of the cool kids who checked me out on pass winked and said, "Burke, use mints, never gum. They will check your breath coming in." With a smile, he had hit the oil too. "Thank you sir, I will remember, mints."

They Gave Me a Pass to Freedom

I packed my few personal civilian items with some gear into my green military issue duffel bag then stashed it under bushes on the perimeter, Friday night after lights out. Nobody saw me stash my gear or come & go from my room.

Confidently casually walking away at 9:00 AM on Saturday morning after being granted a pass to town with a midnight curfew, instructed to use mints, freedom stepping over a curb. I knew they wouldn't miss me until morning. A good head start was all I needed while walking a couple three miles to the I-70 Interstate.

Stuck out my thumb hitchhiking west in my civvies thinking let the universe take care of my needs. It took eleven minutes to catch my first ride escaping Salina, Kansas from the fourth car heading west.

Fuck West Point, to hell with being a warrior in space. Understanding how thermonuclear bombs work, igniting hydrogen and other simple physics-related stuff didn't mean I wanted to build or operate those murdering monstrosities.

I really didn't like the idea of killing people for a living. At the end of the day that's what the military industrial complex does, perfect job for that pyromaniac, Private Fucko. I wanted to work for a 'Think Tank' like Dad's friends took me to once in a while, coming up with ideas for cool stuff. Thought leadership for peaceful living.

Visualizing a perfect blue Pacific Ocean in my mind, heading toward the sunset over a California beach, being anywhere but fucking Kansas. Everything was flat, people carried spit cups for chewing tobacco juice, all they ate was meat, potatoes, and stacks of white bread.

Zero intellectual conversations, certainly nothing esoteric, was being left behind. I'm just glad I didn't end up a crispy critter in a dorm fire being laughed at by some sick psycho killer as his random victim.

Hearken the Gryphon: Time is a cruel joke played on sleeping mankind.

Chance Meeting at Col Mosby's Ditch

Six and a half hours of thumbing & walking three rides west of Salina, chain smoking Camel filters. I couldn't find a pack of Philip Morris Commanders for the life of me anywhere in Kansas.

I looked at a green & white highway sign that read: WALDO, KANSAS POPULATION 14. Across a dust-covered oiled gravel road they called a highway, there was a large six foot plus round sawmill blade stuck into a big barn-wood hand-painted sign; 'Emmett's Saw Shop &Liars Bench'.

A couple of old farmer-looking types in bib overalls were smoking & drinking coffee or beer. I was just trying to figure out what they were drinking. They checked me out but didn't pay attention; one of the patrons had dropped me off, mumbling something about Colonel Mosby's men buried in a ditch beside that black oil and gravel country road.

About forty-five minutes passed without a single car driving by, when a beat up 1966 Gran Torino slows & pulls up as I stuck out my thumb. The driver just stopped in the middle of the road and got out of the car, asking, "Do you know how to drive?"

Looking at this clean-cut runaway up and down, I nodded yes.

He spit onto that black, oily dusty road looking at me dead-eyed. "You gotta driver's license?"

I could see he was dead tired, half drunk, and my ticket the fuck out of Waldo, Kansas.

"I've been driving since I was six, no ten, stole my first car at fourteen, got a learners permit from California, but it's expired." Cool as a cucumber, I hit that Camel filter and looked him back in the eyes.

"Good enough for me. I'm Butch, you're driving." With that he popped around into the passenger door, motioning me to jump in as he opened a bottle of beer.

I tossed my duffel bag in the back seat and slid into the driver's seat. Butch handed me that beer and then slumped into his seat, mumbling, "Wake me up before we get to Dodge City."

Butch started to snore in a dead man returning to Doge sleep like one of Colonel Mosby's men buried over yonder in that ditch.

Smiling, I waved at the fat farm boys on the liars bench, flicked that Camel out the window onto that oily gravel road. Pulling that dirty old Gran Torino into gear thinking I ain't ever coming back to this dead man's ditch bank. Ain't never have, neither, you know what I mean.

I was driving 75-80 mph when Butch Waters woke up with a jolt out of a dead man returning to Dodge City sleep, like one of Colonel Mosby's men in that ditch. "Turn here, damn it, turn now," he barked, exactly like my dad did at the Underground City gate.

Pavlov's dog kicked in automatically and I pulled that dirty 1966 Gran Torino sharp left, kicking up gravel in a lonely dirt parking lot next to a wheat field. Sliding sideways as directed by parking gods into the cool spot, I slid to a stop and slammed it into park.

Hustling Pool in a Ghostly Dodge City Saloon

A *whirlwind of dust enveloped us; we were perfectly parked next to a long white Cadillac. As the dust settled, my eyes revealed a timeworn old neon sign hanging over a cowboy bar complete with hitching post, boardwalk, porch, swinging doors, seeping old timey country music out of its pores.*

Inside this roadside honky tonk, smoke-filled with a long bar, thirty-five cent beers, and featuring a walk the floor steel guitar country singing band playing, 'I'm So Lonesome I Could Cry.' It felt like Hank Williams Senior in the flesh singing for his supper in bumfuck Kansas as we walked through that swinging barroom door.

This young academy runaway looked around noticing the place was full of beer drinking redneck cowboys who were going to kick my long-haired hippie ass. The goofiest looking motherfucker in the room walked up with buck teeth and a shit-eating grin. He looked me in the eye and said, "That's a mighty fine cow skin. Where didja get that, boy?"

I was dumbfounded and merely looked at him, remembering my military school buzz cut, and replied, "My daddy bought it for me at an estate sale in Pasadena…" which was true. He slapped me on the back and said in a country drawl, "Let me buy you a beer and tell me 'bout it. Hank fucking Williams is playing our shithole bar, better than ole Buck

Burnett." In a smooth practiced motion, he spit a slug of Kansas cud juice into a beer bottle held in his left hand.

I was quickly pulled by Butch Waters, who said, "Follow my lead. I've gotta game going."

He pulled me away over toward a pool table with a sleazy looking Indian who had a feather in his black hat, a fat redneck farm boy, and a cowboy-ish looking character with a hundred-dollar hat on his head.

Butch turned to me innocently asking, "Do you know how to shoot pool? What's your name again?"

Standing in that Dodge City honky tonk, smelling of stale smoke mixed with cheap beer, those same pool hall fluorescent lights over pool tables. It instantly brings me back to Pasadena Evening High School, PE classes these past two years studying under a Math PHD Mormon pool shark, teaching geometric shot analysis at Jerry's Family Billiards downstairs near Old Town.

Imagine shooting pool while being taught geometry as high school physical education class. This runaway renegade monk when asked if he could shoot pool quietly said in a very low-key voice, "Yeah, a little bit I reckon, it's Billy."

Butch stared communicating a quickly intense message of 'wrong answer' into my eyes at the mention of a real name then an incorrigible transformation took place. I said in that basement pool hall persona, I'm too cool for school, low key voice. "The name is Frank, Frank Discussion from Waylon, New Mexico."

Feeling like a new person has taken over this seventeen-year-old body less than twelve adventurous hours into my new life.

The fat mark eyeballing these two as he is chalking his pool cue spits out, "Y'all here for introductions or to shoot pool?" He pulled a wad of cash out of his pocket and peeled off a $20 bill from the top.

Butch placed a $20 on the table motioning for the two rubes and Frank Discussion to ante up. I'm thinking I hope he is good, as good as me at least. Risking one of my saved to run away from Military school $45 a week allowance $20 bills, making it $80 laying on the table for this game.

Fatboy redneck grabbed the cue ball saying, "I shoot first." While placing his cue ball into position, a country bar waitress brought us a pitcher of beer, two glasses, looking at me. "That'll be $1.50."

I peeled off two $1 bills, handed them to her, saying "Keep the change."

I heard Butch exclaim with a happy squeal in his voice. "Scratch on the break! We win! Yee the fuck haw!" He quickly grabbed our winnings off the corner of table. Butch sauntered across the barroom grinning, flashing that cash. "You are good luck, Frank Discussion here ya go." He handed me a pair of twenty-dollar bills which I quickly pocketed.

The rubes said it wasn't fair, whining and bitching they wanted another game. Butch told them, "Double or nothing. Y'all here for introductions or to shoot pool?" Now there was $160 on the pool table in that shit hole bar on the outskirts of Dodge City, Kansas.

A voice from the fat boy's peanut gallery floated across the room, "Waylon, where the fuck is Waylon? Sounds like we got the ghost of Hank Williams singing here tonight."

With that a clear sound of a steel guitar and a shrill voice of a very drunk man crackled through a shitty PA system. "I'm walking the floor over you..." I thought about that long white Cadillac we had parked next to in Butch's 1966 Gran Torino.

After fleecing the rubes we drove to a little town. Butch hooked me up with a job as a $12.50 an hour millwright's helper on a huge natural gas compressor, you know, oil field boomtown work. Next he got me, as Frank Discussion, set up with a room in a $35 a week hotel in Ulysses, Kansas that gave workers credit on meals and smokes until payday. He told me to use credit, hide my cash to act broke in front of other workers to set them up for short cons. Short cons were fun and profitable. He taught me lots of things about life.

Butch, it turns out, was a two-bit hustler con man who took a liking to Frank Discussion, showed me the ropes along with tricks to use on the road. He never got caught, never did a day in jail. Butch was what they call a natural, said I was too.

It was an intensive six-week junior con man survival of the fittest course, one of my most interesting educational experiences in life.

My favorite short con that still works to this day is... The ring, the watch, the pigeon drop, lemon drop, all short cons. Two things I learned from Butch that hold true: The basis of any good con is greed, and in a confusing situation, the man who knows what he wants usually gets it.

When we hustled pool I felt like it was honest work. I used math and steady shots to fleece the rednecks.

Kansas conman classes were a lot more fun than that fucking French horn at JPL. Enough background on my previous six weeks. You probably want to hear tales about Oppenheimer's car.

Still, ya gotta love a simple, well-educated short con. Heck, those are stories for another day, if you're lucky. Some things we simply never talk about, the code.

It wasn't the Drugs; it was the lack of them.

*H*earing *the first winter snowstorm of the season was rolling in, I hitched a ride from one of my oilfield coworkers; Cowboy Bob, in a 1967 Barracuda, who drove 55 miles an hour drinking beer non-stop, listening to country music radio all the way to San Bernardino.*

Man, Cowboy Bob was the epitome of a redneck, kept talking about how he hated pot smoking hippies. Every time he did, I thought about the two joints I had in my pocket and how much I wanted to smoke one. Instead I grabbed yet another one of his endless cooler filled with cheap beer we drank, listening to old timey country music on the AM radio, heading into the sunset.

He dropped me off in San Berdoo at the bus station. A $3.43 Greyhound bus ride took me to Hollyfuckingwood, where I spent my first night back in a cheap motel on Vermont above Sunset Boolyvard.

Dad's $2 tip trick, just the tip ma'am, two bucks with a please, in exchange for a late afternoon checkout worked again like always, giving time for a day at the pool after a good night's sleep in a clean fresh bed.

As Frank Discussion, I enjoyed swimming in that motel pool all morning, drinking coffee, eating deli sandwiches and treats from that Opera singing deli place all day. This felt like I was truly back home lying in 86-degree California sunshine on a chaise lounge as Dodge City, Kansas was being smothered with four feet of snow. Saint John's Military School was snowed in six feet according to extrapolation of weather maps shown on the news. Hot California sun beating on my face brought back a feeling of belonging, yet something was missing.

It wasn't the drugs; it was the lack of them. Next stop was retrieval of my buried drug cache in the Doctor's backyard that her kids didn't know about. A short RTD bus trip from Hollyfuckingwood Boolyvard dropped this runaway renegade outlaw monk off on Linda Vista where the old Pasadena old money was well entrenched.

Slipping in their back gate, a small garden trowel was stashed in the shed where I had left it several months earlier. I made short work of getting back that ammo can filled with a variety of drug goodies.

Quickly consuming a small vial containing ten hits of liquid Caltech steam tunnel LSD-25 for equilibrium, I decided to pay the Fields brothers a visit down the cul-de-sac to score a pound or two of fresh weed while figuring out my next move. Where was I going to go after turning down my appointment to West Point and preplanned life of war? There had to be something better than killing people for a living.

Santa Ana winds were blowing hot down the Arroyo Seco. Over the Devils Gate and flowing up Chula Vista Place, bathing a ten hit L-25 Caltech's finest, engulfing Frank Discussion in LSD infused cloak of radioactive psychedelic energy. After running away from Military school in Kansas six weeks earlier, I was finally back in my hometown stomping grounds, coming on hard to this pure LSD.

Seated on a balcony terrace overlooking the Rose Bowl, I, Billy Burke as seventeen-year-old Frank Discussion, watched a craft from the center of this modern Roman Arena rise. It twirled as if it were a ginormous alien spacecraft eighty-six stories high.

A blast of hot LSD infused wind drifted my mind back to that fateful night. The night I was riding in Oppenheimer's car as the only vehicle cleared to leave some remote Nevada base.

It was that night on the remote top secret Nevada 'test range' I was bestowed the distinction of being the only human child in a hush hush super-secret program to be labeled 'incorrigible' and kicked out instead of lobotomized. It was the first and only midnight rejection from the project(s) for being too much trouble.

I was a total pain in the ass in the underground city with that teleportation contraption, when they made me ride home with the big man, Oppy, you know, J. Robert Oppenheimer, father of the atomic bomb, rootie-toot-toot.

That was over 10-years before the fateful night I decided it was time to go full outlaw after escaping military school. Saint John's Military Academy in Salina, Kansas issued a four-state APB whenever a student ran. Good thing I was now six states away.

Stealing Oppenheimer's car would require planning and a certain level of brilliance. One must realistically consider 'men in black' type characters; they were amongst the most feared lawmen. What would give me that juju, the mojo for an all-access pass to life?

Frank Discussion was born from the imagination of Billy Burke November 1975 while on the run from Saint John's Military School in Salina, Kansas. Justice for the rich and rocket scientists with an off the chart genius IQ problem child, rejected as incorrigible from one of the most secret government programs to ever exist in US history.

Back to Chula Vista

*R*eturning *to California landed me back amongst my old Chula Vista buds. Pasadena old money kids, they still live there and are still totally cool. They all got it – running away from a private school; winter was coming on so Frankie Fields graciously offered. "Why not use the beach house at the Rincon in La Conchita? You've been there."*

He continued telling me about the setup, "...The past 3 times anyone has been there, they say it looks like someone has been partying in there, beer cans, roaches and messy beds." Looking at me a smile broke across his face, "Maybe you can party with them; just let them know the rules, daisy chain invitation only."

He gleefully tossed me the keys, as we were all in LSD induced bliss. "You're on your own getting there, Billy. It's the fucking Ventura/Santa Barbara county line, best winter surfing in the golden state."

I could not believe my good luck, thinking, I've now got a place to stay, $772.86 cash, along with a green military duffel bag to go with my short haircut. How do I get to the beach house and around once I'm there, it's Bumfuck Egypt?

The only thing that came to my mind was an unfathomable idea: walk up the street around the corner then steal Oppenheimer's car.

The idea of stealing Oppenheimer's car was one I dare not speak aloud in this den of old Pasadena trust fund money. They gave me an empty remote beach house for the winter right when lying low was most advisable.

Fuck it, I'm stealing Oppenheimer's car. He leaves the keys under the front seat. It's got that magic "Doohickey" that seemed to make us go invisible doing 150 MPH back from the secret underground city that night long ago

.

Yea fuck it, I'm stealing Oppenheimer's car.

*I*t's complex because the old man is the absent-minded *professor who does not miss much. Besides, last I heard he's still dead. His weakness was smugness of living in his 'secret house' up the hill in that quiet Linda Vista neighborhood reserved for old money, knights of industry, and national heroes. The fact it was a short electric car ride in the tunnels under Devils Gate dam, JPL leading to Caltech and the netherworlds is another adventure in itself. Those are Oppenheimer's stories, not Frank Discussion's.*

Oppenheimer's car, a yellow early 1960s station wagon with woody sides that were connected to what the doctor called a "Doohickey" device. It seemed all my father's "friends" on the projects used code names for everything. They got really pissed when I started cracking their codes for sport at age five to six just to see the disturbed looks on their faces.

Insolence has always been my favorite flavor in life.

You see, I'm that kid who was a NASA brat smack dab in the middle of what they call "conspiracy theorist" government projects. They always seemed to make extra 'classes' the norm to me after discovering 167 IQ. They were always throwing weird shit at me, like making student of paranormal science(s), ancient languages, and folklore, taught as science amongst other things. They had me feeding back prodigal childish observations for intellectual consumption via subterfuge of our blue planet's most brilliant scientific thought leaders.

Oppenheimer is famous for giving zero fucks about anything other than what he is focused on at the moment. This car had been specially hand built to protect his absent-minded high-speed driving habits. Transporting the occupants using technological advances that are unknown to this day how it really all works.

Oppenheimer routinely drove like a maniac 70 to 150 MPH while not really paying a lot of attention to the roads. During my 'Incorrigible' ride, I noticed that we seemed cloaked with invisibility. He didn't slow down for a single gate leaving the most secret facility on the planet. Oppenheimer's car drove itself through all types of tight situations, past security checkpoints as if it had a mind of its own. Other drivers, police cars, fire trucks, and delivery vans, nobody seemed to notice us. Riding in Oppenheimer's car while the Doctor was driving with two fingers, smoking like a chimney, lost in thought staring, while puffing most of the time screaming past other cars like they were standing still.

What the fuck is up with this radioactive Geiger counter thumping car that looks like grandma's station wagon? The acid is creeping up my legs, through me gullet, up the back o' my spine into my brain.

They will never catch me in Oppenheimer's car. Shit, it will probably take them a month to even notice it's gone, if ever.

I thanked the Fields for the keys and asked if there is anything special to know about the beach house. They said you'll get visitors once in a while; our secret guest password is "Daisy Chain". Only a handful of people know so you'll have the place pretty much to yourself until Memorial Day. You might want to pick up a surfboard along the way.

Thanking them, grabbing my duffel bag that had a pint of pure Caltech L-25, a pound of top shelf bud they had just sold me for $50, a variety of pills prescribed for a plethora of ailments from my cache at the doctor's house down the street. The medicine bag was full; I have a place to stay rent free for almost six months. Frank Discussion started walking up Linda Vista toward the Lab or JPL Deep Space control center (amongst other things) and Oppenheimer's secret house.

The dirty deed

It was a little after 9:00 PM with hot Santa Ana winds blowing psychedelic visions before my eyes while walking up the Arroyo. I walked past Salvia Canyon up Linda Vista wondering where that craft leaving the Rose Bowl was heading to tonight. A crow with glowing red trinities eyes flew overhead screaming, "DO IT! DO IT!!" Black wings flapping hard 'n steady into this windy enchanted Arroyo Seco night.

My bones were vibrating; it felt like a new adventure was beginning, turning left starting up the hill. Oppenheimer's stay in their 'secret' house that was state of the art modern in 1958 when it was built presumably by Caltech while he was working there. The house is situated on the side of a hill with nothing that can be built above, as if it were a strategic fortress location. The car was always parked in the driveway, unlocked with the keys under the front seat.

My mind felt like it was melting with hot wind when I spotted a glimpse of Oppenheimer's car. It was sitting on a perfect Government Issue concrete pad with room for four cars, while only two occupied it. Quickly sprinting up the ivy-covered hill to the yellow station wagon with the moveable woody sides, Frank Discussion looked himself in the eye from LSD enhanced reflection a few contemplative moments. With my hand on the door, I said to myself out loud, "This is going to change your life in ways you can't even imagine, especially if you get caught. Frank Discussion never gets caught; it's Frank Discussion from here on."

Fuck it, I'm stealing Oppenheimer's car, as I gently pushed the door handle and quietly pulled the door open. An interior light came on. I knew it's now or never, do or die as Frank Discussion reached down, quickly picked up the key from under the seat, then deliberately inserted myself into a new life by pushing that key in the ignition.

With a single flowing movement, I tossed my GI duffel bag across the front passenger seat. Pulling the shifter into Neutral, I pushed with my back against the door jamb, thanking Doctor Oppenheimer for a perfectly level parking area. Jumping in to brake and get ready for the roll down the driveway when Oppenheimer's dog started barking from a dark, unseen location.

"Arf-arf-arf."

Quietly as Frank Discussion could, "Shhhh, Schotzi, it's just me", while pushing the car silently forward onto the downhill sloping white concrete driveway.

The dog chirped like a songbird then was silent, as a thousand sunburst sparkles showered from a giant California great oak tree in the backyard to accompany this just above silent shush.

At the cantilever point, scenes of that secret base flashed in my mind. I thought, here is my Rubicon. There is no going back to the life of wars & college planned for Billy Burke. Frank Discussion took over my personality completely. I jumped in pulling the door shut, making the interior light turn off. The colors were amazing, the driveway started to pulse a bit like heartbeat wavy ground movements. It's just the acid thumping to the drumbeat in my mind.

Silently rolling down Oppenheimer's steep driveway, I'm poised to make the perfect left turn down the hill. A slight thump over a driveway gutter, it made an eerie creaking sound. In the rearview mirror, a white gloved, Mickey Mouse hand on a stick arm, reached from the driveway as if waving goodbye. I nosed the car downhill, nothing but the Santa Ana wind rustling random hallucinations through my brain.

Rolling under a canopy of ancient California live oaks overhanging this street like a tunnel, a dry hot Santa Ana wind blowing, incorrigibly I turned the key to Oppenheimer's car. It roared to life. Something strange happened. Lights came on; the car sped up, took over, turned left on Linda Vista Ave. and accelerated to over 100 MPH in less than a mile to the Devils Gate turn.

I was tripping balls all ten (2000 microgram each) hits of pure liquid Caltech LSD 25 were fully kicked in by now. Oppenheimer's car headed toward a stop sign on Linda Vista and turned right doing 111 freaking miles an hour.

The yellow woody granny wagon made that turn without squealing or feeling any G forces. Its tires zipped over the bridge, turned onto the Devil's Gate dam, then Oppenheimer's fucking car stopped. Lights were on, engine running, it just stopped dead center over what we NASA brats know as the Devil's Gate directly below this exact spot.

The mirrors alerted me, bright flashing red lights of a county Mounties squad-car racing toward me as fast as deputy dawg can drive. "Holy shit, the fucking cops and I haven't gone two miles!" flashed into my brain as I'm becoming aware of another strange sensation, as hallucinogenic illumination of police lights skimmed across the Devils Gate lakes' frog infested waters.

The Earth itself started to vibrate as a section of the bridge grate started to open before Frank Discussion's eyes. Flashing lights were closer. Should I run, jump, hide, beg, oh, that wind feels good on my face.

That sheriff zoomed past me like I wasn't even there, continuing into a windy Norte Dena night call, probably a pimp beating his bottom bitch.

Looking toward **Jack Parsons Lab** with that hot wind bathing me like bath water. Looking down I noticed a small red light above a toggle switch with a red label marked "Doohickey". ON above OFF below, it was on. Hmmm switching the toggle down to OFF the light went off. My foot had been on the gas pedal making Oppenheimer's car jump as control was given to this startled driver trembling on the damn dam.

Quickly slamming on the brakes, I whipped a gangster U on that narrow bridge with deputy Dawgs flashing bubble gum machine barely in my rearview mirror.

Plan: Heading up back streets in La Canada above JPL toward Angeles Crest Highway to complete my getaway.

Incorrigible Frank Discussion passed Billy's old High School thinking of the graduating class I'd miss next June. While turning left across from the Flintridge Riding Club and Oak Grove Park looking directly at the sparkling lights of **Jack Parsons Lab**, my only thought was, I just stole Oppenheimer's car and got away with it … or did I?

Road to the Rincon Escape from LA

I drove through a maze of twisting, turning quiet residential streets until turning up Angeles Crest Highway pushing Oppenheimer's car over the hills and away from that 'secret house' in Pasadena's Arroyo Seco. Next thing I was, driving up that windy mountain road knowing every crack in the concrete from skateboarding down 'The Crest' for years at high speed, without squealing a tire.

Stopping at Vista Point, which is a turnout to view a flowing, glowing sea of lights from our city of lost Angels below; this is where Ray El Ray and I started our downhill Angeles Crest long-board skating runs on homemade high-speed sticks back in 19 and 72. I parked in the perfect 'Vista Point' spot featuring a perfect view of the sprawling twinkling megalopolis before me, tripping hard.

A strong rainbow of light emanating from the Rose Bowl, reaching upward, melding color spectrum infinitely reaching space bound. Above the lights of Los Angeles twinkling like so many lost souls searching for meaning, personal validation, along with their next mortgage payment.

Absorbing this expansive sea of lights, thinking, I'm not going to be one of those saps working at Lockheed or the Lab forty years, only to be rewarded with a shitty watch, a small pension to fritter away while waiting to die. There has to be more to life than working without tasting the rainbow skies, invisible to [sic] normies.

This wind is actually hotter at the summit than it was walking to Oppenheimer's. There is a clarity that comes from LSD infused desert air blowing across our dying granite mountain range.

Bre'r Trinitite Crow Blesses my Journey

A giant crow with trinitite eyes flew into the wind, out *of the darkness at my eye level over the mountainside. This mystical black-winged creature looked directly into my eyes, crowing, "I am your messenger... Caw. Oppenworlds." Flying as hard as it could my winged guardian kept screaming, "Oppenworlds," at 100 MPH, then broke hard left about four feet from my face, landing on a hillside above the car.*

A startled Frank Discussion blurted out, "Crow that was amazing. I am at a crossroad of life…"

Bre'r crow spoke in an other-worldly voice. "That's why we are here to let you know, regardless of the path you take, it will never be alone. CAW!"

Questioning my actions aloud, speaking to a mystical crow with trinitite eyes. "I feel like I just did a very bad thing stealing Oppenheimer's car instead of hitchhiking to the beach house." Shaking my head from side to side as if in shame of my actions, the dirty deed.

Bre'r crow, in an eerie hallucinogenic enhanced voice with its piercing glowing red eyes, spoke. "Frank liberated a thing destined for evil beyond, beyond, what its old owner created, Caw No Evil. No Evil."

"Caawww!" As crow pointed his head toward the desert side of this mountainous divide they were perched upon. "It's yours, CAW watch. Oppenworlds, a caw."

Frank Discussion followed the crow's glowing eyes as its head pivoted changing direction. Watching illuminated light of an atomic bomb distantly exploding over the arid desert. Irradiated light intensified as a nuclear mushroom cloud began to form. I was mesmerized at the unexpected sight of an atomic flash lighting up our night skies brighter than the brightest daylight I've ever seen.

Bre'r crow continued as if he were imparting a message of utmost importance. "You are truly at a crossroads of good and evil with blessings from Oppenworlds. Journey well, caw, journey well... A caw, Oppenworlds."

With that Bre'r crow lifted its wings and flew this time with the wind, across the highway toward the rainbow of lights over the Rose Bowl. As I gazed toward a giant-colored spacecraft descending down this spiraling rainbow light train into the bowels of the Rose Bowl, my mind drifted.

Thinking, hiding a spacecraft in a football stadium is as ballsy as it gets... fuck those assholes. I have a chance to be cool. Looking over at Oppenheimer's car, an old yellow granny wagon with those weird woody sides that moved like aircraft wings sideways, split ways, weird ways.

My eyes drifted again toward Palmdale. Light of the atomic blast seemed to be fading a bit. Thinking if I punch it through the back way, I'll be over the pass on the road to La Conchita before any fallout gets there.

Time to get the fuck out of Dodge, I thought, starting Oppenheimer's car a second time, headed down the pass into a new life as Frank Discussion. Driving past an experimental forest down the hill toward that purple glowing irradiated light over the mountains I felt like top of the world, Ma.

Zooming and zipping that Palmdale cutoff, its downhill four lanes of mountain road all alone, I lit a smoke. That winding mountain road slims into two lanes, leading to a tunnel at Hidden Springs. Driving through this magical tunnel was like a Disneyland hallucinogenic experience to say the least. It felt like two hours traversing a 200 yard long hole through solid granite rock. Tripping balls like a motherfucker.

Oppenheimer's car entered that high mountain tunnel as my interior seemed to light up like a hallucinogenic theme park. Each rock was glowing, a different color of the rainbow over a shimmering roadway. I could differentiate the veins of ore pulsating out a golden glow from within the Earth. An iridescent tunnel started to breathe like lungs dripping liquid light that splattered in front of me on the road like translucent glowing drops of oxygenated life.

A big drop of life hit my windshield, exploding a glowing liquid rainbow of flavorful colors. Truly an unexpected, unanticipated deliciously large, psychedelic splash of life flavored energy. I'm wondering if it tastes as good as it looks.

I slowed down and was looking for the windshield wiper switch when all of a sudden, out of the tunnel.

The Country Punk Hitchhiking Cowgirl

*O*n the other side of Hidden Springs tunnel there is a single street light along fourteen miles of desolate mountain to desert highway. A chick with flowing brunette hair under a cowboy hat, her dress whipping in the wind revealing beautiful legs, adorned with brown cowboy boots, was centered in a circle of light. She smiled and stuck out her thumb looking me in the eyes, then winked. I instinctively pulled over to pick her up.

The country punk hitchhiking cowgirl opened the door with a smile saying, "Hi, I'm Sheila headed to Camarillo. How far you going?"

She slid in with a small backpack, carefully placing it on the floor between her legs. She closed the door as we pulled away from that iridescent circle of light.

"Frank Discussion here, I'm headed to the Rincon at La Conchita," I said while looking at a spectrum of the rainbow bleeding out of a radiation cloud which came back into sight as we rounded a curvy bend above Hidden Springs. Riding with a beautiful woman comfortably seated in Oppenheimer's car.

Sheila smiled a knowing smile, pulling out a cigarette, placing in between her lips, asking. "Gotta light, cowboy?"

At this I broke into a grin while digging a Zippo out of the open ashtray. Flicking that lighter open, noticing some sort of symbol while holding it, saying, "Anything for you, Sheila." Lighting her cigarette filled the car with the smell of Ronson lighter fluid and Marlboro red swirling about.

"La Consweeta? Rincon? What's up with that, some sort of a music festival?" came from a demure Sheila, who was sizing me up from a hitching girl's perspective.

I put my foot into the gas, guiding Oppenheimer's car down Angeles Forest Highway, passing the Mount Emma Road at a comfortable 90 climbing to 110 MPH. "I've got a place at the beach for the winter on the Ventura/Santa Barbara county line. It's called the Rincon. Hear its good surfing and quiet this time of year."

Sheila was settling into the car, brushed her hair back using the passenger mirror on the sun visor. She looks outside at what is now becoming high desert, Joshua tree darkness. Leaning back taking a big drag of her Marlboro with piercing eyes locked on me said "You know, we should dance. There is a place I want to stop along the way."

Then Sheila became aware of an atomic mushroom cloud blowing in from the open Mojave Desert toward our direction. "What the fuck is that?"

I pushed Oppenheimer's car over 125 MPH and a green light above the "Doohickey" switch lit up, catching my passenger's attention. Looking at the atomic mushroom backlit by the iridescent nuclear blast glowing large in the distant sky, I said, "Dancing is good if we can get away from the Oppenheimer cloud in time." Lighting a Philip Morris Commander, I glanced at the lighter Caltech JPL symbol with Roman numerals XXI etched held to a vision of an atomic glowing cloud coming closer as the car hurtled towards it.

The Oppenheimer Doohickey

"Are you tripping or what?" Sheila asked casually reaching down unconsciously and flicked the "Doohickey" switch into its 'on' position. Why people like to flick switches on and off is beyond me but she did.

The green light immediately went out as a red light came on. The sound in the car changed from V-8 engine into an electric humming sound eerily much lower in volume as our speed picked up to the point that landscape outside the window blurred like a fast motion movie.

Oppy's car took control again, turning hard left 90 degrees at the next paved desert road. I looked at Sheila, who looked at me, out the window then over to its speedometer reading 222 MPH and climbing. The needle was only a quarter of the way up, speedometer looking like it was from a jet or spacecraft, something fast, yet an old round analog dial thing-a-ma-jig..

"500 Miles per hour! I said dance with me, don't kill me! What are those Roman looking numbers?" Sheila looked confused but not scared and slowly continued. "I must be tripping hard from that last hit. What the fuck is up with your car?" She took a drag that seemed to inhale the tail end of her Marlboro while looking at the mushroom cloud moving away at a very rapid pace.

I reached down, flicking on the radio, which crackled to life with a mechanical voice.

"Lawrence Livermore safety chamber, auto tracking engaged." The radio lit the sound of the car up with Merle Haggard singing.

"We don't smoke Marijuana in Muskogee, we don't take our trips on LSD; we don't burn our draft cards down on Main Street, 'cause we like living right and being free."

A mechanical humanized voice sounded out over the crystal-clear music "Fourteen seconds to chamber drive engagement, re-state desired destination."

Sheila blurted out. "I wanna dance Shady Dave's Hideaway, Dawson Drive, Camarillo."

The control room voice responded, "Destination Shady Dave's Hideaway, Dawson Drive at Barry Street, Camarillo California, present time; prepare for engagement."

Frank Discussion looked very disturbed asking Sheila, "What are you doing?" As the car immersed into a rainbow of light, electric whining sound intensified with a feeling of dropping in an elevator. These two tripping passengers could see nothing but colors, light floating fantasmical cloud, surrounding Oppenheimer's car. Yet we felt comfortably enveloped in warmth of this new energy infusion.

Over the radio Merle Haggard sings his current hit single. *"We don't make a party out of loving; we like holding hands and pitching woo..."*

Instinctively grabbing onto each other's hands looking at each other as the interior of Oppenheimer's car turned a hard deep purple. A psychedelic cloud floating furiously in a peaceful manner then a glimpse of what looked like a large crow with trinitite eyes, flapping through a purple mist. Then...

Silence surrounds us in place of any clouds, purple is gone, the car is perfectly parked facing a faded flashing neon sign reading Shady Dave's (the big S was burnt out) with HIDEAWAY in large white neon letters flashing to a heartbeat of country music pulsating through its barn wood walls.

I reached down casually flipping the "Doohickey" switch into its off position silencing music, our car, lights, everything stopped cold.

"Please don't touch the controls; I'm still learning how to drive this car." Trying to be as cool and calm as possible considering the acid, the crow, cops, atomic blast, while the fact we are now riding in Oppenheimer's stolen car sank into this person rechristened 6-weeks ago as, Frank Discussion, just experienced my first baptism under fire. I'm still tripping hard on 20,000 micrograms of pure liquid Caltech LSD.

"I just want to get drunk, dance… I've got forty-two bucks, after that ride the drinks are on me," Sheila said while opening the door not thinking about traveling eighty-six odd miles in under $4/10^{th}$ of a second.

"Dancing's good, what kind of show!" asking quickly, exiting the car thinking about that hot ass wiggling across the parking lot, quickly catching up to her outside a pair of swinging saloon doors, familiar sounds of a honky-tonk drifting into my ears.

Sheila just got a big mischievous grin. "You are gonna [sic] like this, like I'm gonna like you. C'mon." As she pushed through the saloon doors, a very white cover band playing Freddie Fender's current hit, "Wasted Days & Wasted Nights", was on stage.

PRESENT DAY HERE & NOW 1975 @ Shady Dave's

Shady Dave's Hideaway swinging bar room doors open effortlessly for the pair as we slide into a country haven in this rural California town a couple hours north of Los Angeles.

I inhale the sights, sounds, and smells from this roadside honky-tonk as if a pirate breathing fresh sea air after escaping the hangman's noose on Barbados.

Following Sheila across a barn wood floor toward a redneck bar, remembering my hair is short. They think I'm one of them. Not a yippie in disguise.

Dichotomy, life will flow to opposite extremes from a hot hippie chick to this hitchhiking country punk. At the end of the rainbow, it's always about her energy, twinkling eyes, mischievous smile, and lips filled with hot delicious kisses. "Two shots of Jack and a pitcher of horse piss beer. Gimme some quarters too." We slid into two empty bar stools at the end of that long smoky bar near a pool table.

The bartender slapped a couple of shot glasses onto the bar, promptly filling them with Lynchburg whiskey. The pair picked them up as Sheila said, "To trouble, let's get into some trouble."

Downing those drinks she slapped hers onto the bar with a crack motioning for more as I heard the distinct sound of a tight rack breaking on the pool table.

I held my hand over the shot glass with a nonverbal 'no' while grabbing a fresh mug of beer. Lighting up a Philip Morris Commander, I turned as if in a trance in this country music smoke filled bar, packed with rubes ready to be fleeced. Invigorated filled with life, ready for adventure, naturally seizing the day. Carpe diem, Billy Bob, carpe that fucking diem you are a free man.

Fleecing the Rubes; a chump change parlor trick.

———◆———

*L*iving on the road as an outlaw changes one's *perspective while naturally honing man skills. I learned the hard way that it's an 'Eat what you kill' world. Man do I like to eat steak and pussy. Neither meal is usually free, when they are always with a catch, a hook, somehow being obliged.*

My outlaw time on the road with Butch became a reality just a few hours after ditching being a candidate for West Point at Saint John's Military Academy in Salina, Kansas. God bless the great state of California with justice for the rich. Juvenile Hall for the poor, but military school for the son of a 'rocket scientist' engineer at JPL aka Jack Parsons Lab or just 'the lab' working on beyond top-secret projects that brought his young son for "classes" and swim time at the ever present government pool.

Scoring in the top 2 1/10ths of 1% in the nation on military entrance exams (ASVAP) was enough to make me want to peace out. I didn't want to push the red kill button; that's what the military industry complex is built for.

Oppenheimer, Tesla, and Einstein created the 'Atomic Bomb' to end war, creating free energy as a byproduct; Management, unfortunately, used their science for greed; Atomic weapon systems cost billions and billions of dollars to build & maintain. Fucking greed driven government contracts for billions to endlessly service those nuclear weapon systems.

Enrolling one's children in lessons for everything seemed to be parents along the Arroyo's credo during that midcentury renaissance era I grew up in. At my high school for geniuses where they taught astral projection next to light and other reality, astrophysics, entrepreneurship, and more. PE or physical education was combined with geometry on a pool table. Pool sharking taught by a black Mormon pool shark with a PhD in Mathematics. Go figure. It's Pasadena's idea of progressive education.

I was good; a gamblers jack dream and worst nightmare at the same time.

Jerry's Family Billiards in Pasadena is where I went to finishing school for shooting pool using mathematical perfection combined with 167 IQ ability used to instantly line up every conceivable combination of shots on a pool table at a glance. Steady hand to eye coordination had something to do with martial arts & archery training since age eleven at the YMCA.

Swimming since age 2, with lessons how to dance at Cotillion, horseback, sailing, rowing, survival, physics, tennis, fencing, debate, how to make LSD, such skills are essentials learned by young Billy Burke during that golden era. Plus we practiced shooting pool in mansions with billiard rooms left over from days of yore. Ya know I still wonder why every pool room in a big house has a barber's chair in it?

Back to the road to the Rincon trip.

Hustling a game of pool here and there had become a way of life with me. I was watching the progress of their game, coolly sliding, over placing a quarter in the coin well behind another. The rubes playing looked, shrugged, the ugly one saying, 'It's five bucks a game here, boy," while chalking his cue like he was a pool shark or hot shit trick shooter. We shall see.

I looked him in the eye calmly asking, "How [sic] 'bout five bucks a ball, cowboy?" This one didn't scratch on the break, they made me earn their money one shot at a time, grinding, measuring, making sure that the tip spun the right English every time, just the tip. Ole Frank Discussion knew to miss a shot here & there so they wouldn't think I was hustling their redneck asses, but I was.

Still tripping balls on those ten hits (2,000 micrograms per hit) of pure liquid Caltech LSD-25 taken on Chula Vista, I fleeced the rubes out of $86.50 and two pitchers of beer.

I had that drunken dance session with Sheila. Man, can she dance.

Romantic overtures fueled with a pocketful of cash; asking politely with an intense kiss if she would like to play my favorite game, just the tip. We fucked the living shit out of each other at her place in every way imaginable. Talked about life, the universe, when we got to the meaning of time I found myself kissing Sheila goodbye as she fell asleep in a psychedelic orgasmic bliss. I decided to continue my journey after leaving her a bedside note with directions & promises to meet again.

Until then, mon amie, the country punk hitchhiking cowgirl, Sheila.

SHORE PATROL LEADS MY PATH TO THE BEACH HOUSE

*H*eading down a predawn foggy Carpentaria highway brought Oppenheimer's car to the coast. Cruising past Rincon point accompanied by a 'Shore Patrol' of pelicans as escort, inhaling Pacific air, a free man with my window down, I felt alive. Pelicans flying majestically directly above, perfect effervescent surf lines on mile long waves welcoming this tired outlaw runaway, renegade monk with a pocketful of liquid LSD driving 'Father of the Atomic Bomb's' stolen car.

Turning left into sleepy La Conchita, slowly driving over train tracks, up to the garage/surf shack in the furthest southeast corner of this sleepy seaside village. Cracked blacktop ended driving over a small ridge onto the highest most remote spot with a small garage framed against a magical sky. Prickly pear cactus behind it, a perfect parking spot unseen from the road, I pulled into it without hesitation.

Feeling alive, 100% complete, parking Oppenheimer's car behind the beach house, arriving with a psychedelic sunrise accompanied by the very welcoming sound of crows on a wire.

Only the sound of surf hitting rocks after I shut off the car, drinking it in, breathing, living, being.

Grokking in fullness of the moment.

It was a day of days.

The day I stole Oppenheimer's car.

Project Morning Glory

Free LSD for the People

Timothy Leary

Tune in, turn on, drop out… Uncle Timothy Leary

This is story about how a band of 60s radicals planted enough FREE LSD to give the entire United States youth free LSD hallucinogenic experiences.

A lasting gift from the evangelism of the 1970s religious, find yourself movement is free LSD for the people of America. Its growing wild in the streets has been for over forty years now.

Many thanks to the Youth International Party (YIPPIEs) made famous with the Chicago 7, who not surprisingly created more changes than given credit for. All by the YIPPIE's design, of course.

It began for me as Frank Discussion with a grizzled hippie aptly named "Old Bear Strongarm". Everyone just called him Bear for short. He was only a few years older than me at the ripe age of twenty-one. Bear tinkered with growing hydroponic marijuana, mushrooms in a cave, and then came upon a scientific study from Sandoz Pharmaceuticals that several types of organic morning glory seeds produce a chemical compound similar to LSD but two to six degrees off from pure Lysergic Acid Diethylamide being a pure burning LSA glyceride compound.

Old Bear Strongarm appeared at the open to the sea door of the beach house late one day as I was watching the sun slip into the Pacific. The beach house was actually a "garage" for tax purposes, yet a small house built with garage doors facing the ocean. It was in the last row up the hill in the corner of this small seaside community.

Old man W.C. Fields had bought the lot for $1,000 on his way back from a nearby winery, something about winning a free set of steak knives. The old man put $25 down on a corner perimeter lot so their family had a beach house. Probably still do.

Old Bear Strongarm smiled and said, "Daisy chain... (recognitive pause) motherfucker, what are you doing here?"

I responded, "House sitting for the winter. We are having a heat wave. C'mon in, tell me a story. Ain't had a Daisy Chain visitor yet..."

Old Bear Strongarm, or Bear for short, grew up a few blocks from my childhood home. Bear's father worked for Lockheed "Skunkworks" developing secret stuff. He was a genius. Bear was excited to see about a pound of pot in a grey busboy bin sitting on the table next to me with a smoldering bong.

Note: This man talks in circles while getting baked on bud. Burnt out dirty wood hippie speak is what I call it these days. I will condense his story for brevity and to save the reader an assault on the English language.

Bear had just driven his Toyota Land Cruiser back from a secret meeting outside of Big Sur with the YIPPIEs. Abbie Hoffman was there with Uncle Tim, Phil Owsley, and leaders of a few LA based cults that he babbled about, but didn't really name.

Daisy Chain Old Bear Armstrong Tall Tale About Ending War

*B*ear was invited because he had successfully cracked the code of how to order and obtain LSD-infused hallucinogenic Morning Glory seeds from bulk seed dealers and made a few batches. Something about the ancient Aztec and Mayan cultures developing the "Heavenly Blue" and "Pearly Gates" variety for shamanistic purposes.

The Yippies came up with a plan to use altruistic hippies, cult kids, environmental do-gooders to unknowingly plant a vast network of small farms that blooms millions of hits of the purest LSD available, all for free. Free LSD growing wild, fresh crop o' seeds every year regardless of whether kids, their parents, or just the birds trip balls.

In plain English, this means that just about any blue or purple morning glory plant you see growing on a hillside backyard as vine, state parks, city parks, beaches, hillsides along thousands of miles of Interstate Highways from San Diego, California to Bangor, Maine, Nevada, Arizona, and New Mexico deep into Texas are blooming each year with the most pure mild LSD available. Just wait till the flowers go to seed, pick, dry, husk, consume, and trip ez-pz.

Freeing people by expanding their minds was the idea.

Can you imagine how radical the idea of ten, twenty, even thirty million people tripping balls at the same time across America would be? The yippie's did, that was their plan.

Wars would end, babies would be born, books written, books read, movies made, love made, music, dancing in the streets like a giant Grateful Dead concert.

FREE LSD IS GROWING EVERYWHERE FOLKS

I just looked at him and said, "Man, you are tripping balls; you mean those weed plants we pulled in that rich lady's garden for extra money get you high?" I shook my head thinking Bear is so full of shit. Here, smoke another bowl, man, handing over a packed pipe.

Bear looked at me with astonishment, saying, "Let's go for a ride." Putting down his pipe, he picked up his hat & jacket.

I pulled the garage doors shut, locked up, and started walking toward Oppenheimer's car wondering, "Why does he want a ride in this? How does he know?"

Honk, honk, honk, honk, the engine of a beat-up white Land Cruiser starts, the buggy lurches as he lets up the clutch while opening the passenger door. "Get in. Let's get a milk shake." As I'm trying to sit down, I pull the door closed trying not fall out as Bear punches it over the bumpy dirt lot toward the paved road.

It's dark by now and there are no streetlights in sleepy La Conchita, most of the summer houses closed for the winter. Bear drove to the next town up, Summerland with an open hamburger stand advertising MILK SHAKES, a small neon light in the window.

Old Bear Strongarm pulled up, kicking up a few rocks, got us two large chocolate milk shakes from the window. Upon returning to the car, he opened a small suitcase that had thousands of small jeweler-sized manila envelopes neatly lined up in rows with separators like a salesman's sample case.

Bear hands me one of his small envelopes, saying, "1/3rd ounce of organic morning glory seeds. We soak the husks off them and separate with a spaghetti strainer. Let the seeds dry a few hours in the coffee grinder, then bam." Smiling, he goes on, "I discovered that 1/3rd of an ounce is about the same as a typical 1,000 microgram of windowpane or that Caltech stuff you get." Bear looks out the window a moment then back at me. "Plus it's clean, pure organic. Wait till you try it."

Just then a CHiP pulled up next to us with two uniformed officers getting out. One glanced at our beat-up white Toyota Land Cruiser fully rigged for off-roading but he was more interested in making a beeline to the men's room.

Bear laughed. "I see the look in your eye. This is legal. You can buy morning glory seeds right there, but those are not organic." Pointing to the hardware store across the street while snapping his small suitcase filled with seed packets closed. "Here you stir it up, doesn't taste bad, doesn't taste good unless it's in a shake."

I said, "I haven't seen anything close to the liquid Caltech L25. They had to close down the lab, teleported the whole thing to Belgium was the story I heard."

I continued to stir with a wooden Popsicle stick. "So you're saying this milk shake will make the walls melt and I'll trip balls?" Looking quizzically like what the fuck is this weird powder going into a perfectly good malted chocolate milk shake?

Old Bear Strongarm laughed. "It takes two for wall melting," dumping the contents from another small envelope into my drink, which was promptly consumed without further question on the bumpy ride down past Rincon Point.

Keep America Beautiful

QUESTION How does one condense four to ten hours of brains dripping out my ears clean cool tripping? We took the dog tunnels under the coast highway to the beach, drawn like moths to a small fire with two topless surfer girls swaying in the moonlight.

Gary, the local strumming surfer, was playing a rendition of Neil Young's "The Needle and the Damage Done" as we approached. Terri and Jenny Node waved in a trance dance tripping balls all night long with beach beauties and ugly motherfuckers alike.

I woke up on the top bunk, peed, then as if in a trance prepared the percolator with morning coffee that filled the Fields' beachfront "Garage" with the aroma of hot java like a needle injecting heroin into a junkie's veins.

A few hours later after several jugs of java and many prime buds smoked, Bear started into what seemed at the time like a farfetched tale that made more sense around every turn. The Youth International Party YIP aka YIPPIEs had a few well-placed agents of mercy planted within all of America's conglomerates. These included landscaping companies utilizing seed manufacturers to implant the Eisenhower Defense Highway System (now known as the Interstates) with flora and fauna to occupy the drivers with a tranquil experience.

Keeping with Lady Bird Johnson's Keep America Beautiful campaign that demanded colorful flowers, Morning Glories were amongst those chosen to be planted along tens of thousands of miles of Interstate Highways from Coast to Coast.

God Bless the Youth International Party! YIPPIE!

*O*ld Bear Strongarm continued with this wild story that came from the lips of a very deep underground thanks to Frank Discussion's first Grand Central Market Meeting with Abbie Hoffman's twisted mind.

Abbie Hoffman and the Technical Assistance Program (TAP), an alternative YIP brain trust made up of Rand Corporation and Caltech rejects or runaways like me, had deduced: If we get 10% of the population, roughly ten to thirty million people, tripping balls on LSD, war would be impossible.

I was absorbing this information while having the stolen car from the father of the atomic bomb sitting outside my runaway paradise beach shack.

I stood up, looked right at Old Bear, asking, "What can I do to help? This plan sounds like it will work." Deep in thought about how exactly do we solve this equation?

Old Bear continued his story. "They are meeting Tony Alamo, Ron Hubbard, with Tim Leary and Baba Ram Doss. Something they call the Los Angeles cult contingent day after tomorrow, get this, on Walt Disney's grave in Glendale at Forest Lawn by the big mausoleum where I dropped you with Raymundo to skate that steep ass hill."

Old Bear started laughing at the thought because I 'ate it' halfway down that run sliding out on water running across a slick, steep, perfect blacktop boneyard road, any skate bombers dream run, at Forest Lawn. "Man, I can still see it. Ray just water skis over that water slick, you the look on your face while going down." He drifts momentarily, hitting his pipe, looking out an open garage door at the ocean continuing, "12:12 High Noon be at Walt Disney's grave, help us figure out an EZ way for cult kids to covertly plant these, man."

I looked at Old Bear hitting that funky pipe of his. "What the fuck do you mean? Those cult guys are kinda heavy duty creepsters."

Old Bear said, "Yeah, Abbie is presenting the how to grow organic peace as a front. They don't have a clue it makes you trip balls, man." Old Bear continued, "Abbie has a way of understanding how people work; he came up with a front to help the environment with a save the planet plant."

Frank Discussion shook his head trying to conceptualize, just blurting out, "Huh, I've got close to a pint of pure Caltech L 25 that doesn't trip as clean as what we did last night, not near as clean. That was the cleanest burn I've ever had in my life." Reminiscing upon my brain dripping out my ears while dancing with Terri Node barefoot in the sand by last night's fire watching light twist the music, grounded by a bass line from the Pacific Ocean itself.

Abbie Hoffman Says; I'd Like to Buy The World A Trip

*O*ld Bear Strongarm just looked at me with a grin like he had shit his pants with a warm turd baking down his leg at a slow pace. The black and white TV blared aCoca-Cola commercial of the era on a shitty UHF snow channel. "Abbie Hoffman would like to buy the world a trip."

Old Bear continued his enchanting tale. "… Abbie said if we bought the world a free trip on LSD, people would stop fighting, no more war, people would think for themselves. It's what the world wants, the real thing LSD is…" Bear snorkeled into a bizarre laugh while gathering his things.

Our question is how do we get millions of people tripping balls at the same time if the drug is totally illegal and the pigs are using it for counterintelligence purposes in Viet Fucking Nam?

Abbie Hoffman solution: let's call cult kids to plant morning glory using a do-gooder story as a cover, then a few years later tell everyone so they go out, harvest it then trip balls. Little did we know this would be kept secret for over forty years, until this now.

Yippies are good at keeping secrets secret.

*W*riter's note:* *Guess what? They are all dead. Once again as Frank Discussion I'm the last man standing, keeping my word or lie to my dead buddies as you shall discover reading my adventures.*

Old Bear went on, saying, "Frank, I need some help with this. We need a way to can plant vines guerrilla style in addition to seed orders we had switched with some state highway landscape contractors."

To make a long story longer, Old Bear gave me his interpretation of the secret meeting, asked me to help think of a plan and help with his part for presentation the day after tomorrow. They tried to work out a stoned overview, but Bear knew Frank would come up with something to make him look good with the TAP gang, more important something to use to end war.

Next thing I knew, Old Bear Strongarm was back in that white Toyota Land Cruiser, spitting fumes n' gravel, headed south on Pacific Coast Highway. Once again I was alone on the Rincon looking down at the telegraph poles, with only crows for company today.

"I was tripping balls, baked on Bud, and jacked up with three pots of strong ass beach coffee. I'm off my Ritalin and focused on one thing…

What would Doctor Oppenheimer do, challenged with providing free LSD for the people to end war?

To settle the internal arguments within myself, I decided to engage in a triple overdose of pure liquid LSD 25 from the Caltech labs. Carefully measuring 10,000 micrograms into a vial as I had so many times before, wondering how this is going to turn out. This one wasn't to dose hundreds of attendees at a DeaD concert; it was for personal consumption to conceptualize a mission plan.

I had been living half high on the hog, the other half eating stolen kale & veggies from unattended winter gardens in this tiny beach community ninety minutes north of Los Angeles. I took two overripe turnips that acted as organic speed, put them in our old glass bar blender and mixed it.

Methodically pouring it into a cheese cloth over a small bucket and straining all the pulp out, I carefully poured its contents back into the blender along with what in 2023 would be considered about 1000 hits of pure liquid LSD 25 from my emergency cache buried by the Doctor's pool on Chula Vista, retrieved the night I stole Oppenheimer's car.

"I've gotta take a leak before I can do this," I said to myself after pouring that vial of LSD into the beet juice before turning on the blender. I walked around the garage facing the small canyon of banana and weed plants then screamed.

YYYYYYYYYYYYYYYYYYYYYYYYYYYYYYYYYYYYAAAAA
AAAAAAAAAAAAAAAAAAAAAAAAAAAAAAAAAAAAAAAA
AAHHHHHHHHHHHHHHHHHHHHHHHHHHHHHHHHHHHHHH

I tried in vain to shake those last three drops after an especially long urination session. Bre'r crow laughed at my urination spectacle.

This is it, I don't know why this is important, but it is, and I'm going for it. Returning to the small piece of wood plank called a bar that substituted for a kitchen in this little beach house runaway paradise, I mumbled something that sounded like "fuck it". I pushed a button on the blender with a higher than high at the time dose of speed mixed with 10,000 micrograms of pure liquid Caltech L-25 of the last steam tunnel batch.

Hoisting a large pewter goblet, I said to bre'r crow sitting on the wire, "Down the mother clucking hatch, my friends, it's now or never, it's do or die… L'chaim, I'll take the high road, you take the low road and we shall meet in forever."

That beet juice was breakfast of champions with a little vitamin LSD added for extra brain food energy. Damn, those seeds were clean. I mean clean like those fairy tale butterflies on the wall. The acid quickly took hold like never before. I could taste purple sky while the crashing waves sent showers of light bathing me in a warm sound of life's sustenance.

Trancelike came the Gryphon

A Cheshire cat of sorts with a top hat, cane, tuxedo complete with tails as if he was living in an animated cartoon. The Gryphon laughed. As he laughed, a flock of birds came flying out of his Kundalini chakra. As his laughter grew, birds came out faster. They swirled above growing larger into a flock. He repeated, "Watch and learn, watch and learn, watch and learn."

"Caw Caw."

With a flap of black feathers, Bre'r crow was back on its power pole perch outside large open garage doors facing the beach.

I was just starting to feel the effects of this LSD-enhanced beet juice as Bre'r crow spoke. "Use the birds dumb ass, use the birds... caw birds, caw birds..."

I just looked at the crow befuddled. "The birds, the birds, caw..."

I was taken over by the urge to shit, like I'm going to crap my pants any moment. What the fuck was I thinking?

The crow took on the voice of an old black Virginia gentleman. "That's right, you 'bout to shit yo pants, boy. Ah ha ha ha ya ha, caw, haw caw caw boy..."

Cutting loose, I farted a big, wet, juicy fart; it felt like brains slipped out my ear as I ran to the small toilet closet called a bathroom on the other end of the garage. Without going into nasty details, relieving myself in a hearty manner, I cleaned up, grabbed the half-finished glass containing remainders of beet juice, sauntering through the living room, wandering out open ocean view garage doors as if in a trance again.

"Caw, you shithead, caw the birds, the birds, the bird shit, dummy, it's all in the poop, you fuckhead," came from that big black Bre'r crow perched on a wooden crossbeam of a very old telegraph pole. Electricity was strung up on to the shack from the street below.

"Caw, morning glory, caw, glory, morning caw, morning, morning, caw, caw, caw…" That crow wouldn't shut up. He kept crowing n' going.

"Birds LSD for people, caw. People, birds shit seeds, elllllesssdeeeeeeeeeeee, caw, free acid, caw, free acid." The crow emitted a visual psychedelic message, with his words turning into visions before my eyes.

I could feel engulfment of this being, as if every pore in my body was in hallucinogenic vibrational harmonic tune, while the crow continued its message. "Cones, pinecones, use pinecones, asswipe, the birds, seeds on cones. Daisy chain yourself, man."

Big black Bre'r crow flapped its wings flying off the pole. "Birds, the birds are your key to free LSD caw, free acid man caw." Flapping its wings into the wind, the magnificent bird rose into a sunless sky. Picture Heckle & Jeckle in top hats, with a stream of birds coming out of their tummies.

What next?

I contemplated the possibilities of how to distribute free LSD to millions of people while tripping balls in this remote beach house after stealing Oppenheimer's car. What did they kick me off that secret project for again? Was it the underground cities LSD adventure or was it...

Epiphany came to me. Pinecones, that motherfucking crow was talking about bird shit, bird shit from seed laced pinecones, it's the key to free LSD for people. Homemade glue like we used in elementary school made with flour mixed into seeds. Simply dip pinecones or roll them in morning glory seed paste, let them dry.

Voila, either they land in a good place, germinate, and grow, or the birds eat the seeds and crap them everywhere, pooping free LSD for the people after the plants grow a minimum of two seasons.

Heavenly Blues and Pearly Gates for the cult kids of Heaven's Gate. Same for the Hubbard crowd and the Tony Alamo gang. If we can get the Knights of Columbus planting these, that would be totally awesome.

Frank Discussion is off to the races, now to find that bag of flour in kitchen cabinets to get started.

YIP Tricks Cults into Project Morning Glory; Free LSD for the People!

It was like old times driving past televangelist "Doctor" Gene Scott's 'House of the Lord' where faithful pilgrims could buy a seat in the house of the Lord for a mere $10,000.

Turning right into Forest Lawn out of habit, I stopped to say a Hail Mary while listening to nursery rhymes playing from a kiddies bone yard, a cemetery playground for dead babies. I slowly drove that old yellow wagon up a very steep hill creeping toward a strange meeting at Walt Disney's grave.

Raymundo and I started many a hit 'n run skateboard bombing down that steep hill after smoking weed at the top, sometimes blasting past somber funeral processions, baked on Bud, or tripping balls.

I parked Oppenheimer's stolen car behind Bear's Land Cruiser near a large ornate mausoleum. There were a variety of people in attendance representing all the major LA based cults with a few Earth First tree hugging type radicals.

Jerry Rubin and Abbie Hoffman ordered an extra-large funeral service tent complete with chairs and refreshments on the grave adjacent to Walt Disney's niche. (Probably paid for it with the Underhill's American Express card)

These guys never cease to amaze me, two of the most wanted anti-war radicals in the country dressed in suits at Forest Lawn, Glendale smoking a joint at Walt Disney's grave next to a green, small circus-sized funeral tent, complete with attendants, seating, refreshments, sound, setup with stage and robed choir.

Spotting Old Bear Strongarm talking with long hairs in suits, I quickly make a beeline over. Hearing them saying "distribution is a bitch; these are hard to plant, then take hold."

A small relatively short haired, conservatively dressed Frank Discussion approached this group. "Bear, Bear I've got it figured out. The crows came to me with the Gryphon…"

Abbie Hoffman, overhearing that statement, looked in my direction then asked, "Billy, you have something?"

Looking him in the eye, I said, "Remember, its Frank, Frank Discussion; yes, the crows showed me how to plant the seeds." With that I pulled what is now called the first Project Morning Glory pinecone out of my bag, handing it off to Abbie Hoffman.

"Pinecones rolled in a simple flour paste like we made in kindergarten so it's edible. Morning glory seeds are mixed into a paste that washes away first rain. If we can make these by the thousands, then drive the roadways everywhere, chuck them out the window, let the birds, bears, and bees do the rest."

Abbie Hoffman, with his long freaky hair tucked into a hat, looked ecstatic as he handed a pinecone to Jerry Rubin. They both started to laugh saying, yes this is it. They also agreed to go with the TAP (Technical Assistance Program) recommendation to infiltrate purchasing departments of the State Highway Administrations in all fifty states.

"I've got about a hundred or so in the wagon ready to go as testers," I informed the gathering. "I get obsessive; they aren't all the same mix but look pretty good."

Heavenly Blues by God, by God, Heavenly Blues @Walt Disney's Grave

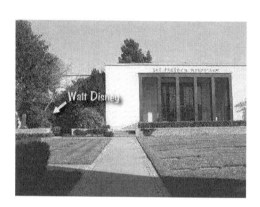

To make a long story longer, the YIPPIEs used Frank Discussion's pinecones in pure Walt Disney graveside street theater. Handing them out to the Whose Who of the 1975 religious leaders based in Southern California.

Accompanied by a bogus "Scientific American" article complete with faked big pharma papers, Project Morning Glory was about to be put into action.

Jerry Rubin & Abbie Hoffman worked that crowd up to YIPPIE infused, religious furor frenzy. At one point Timothy Leary jumped to his feet, hands in the air, singing, "Praise the Lord, save the Earth, praise the lord, save the Earth." Within seconds the crowd erupted into a tent revival meeting complete with an electric organ led by the COGIC

(Church of God in Christ) contingent from Altadena singing it old timey-like.

"Praise the Lord, Pass the Morning Glory Seeds, Heavenly blues by God." Timothy Leary got the robed COGIC choir going full gospel style.

"Heavenly blues, by God, by God, heavenly blues by God."

It was a frenzied chorus wild with the Holy Spirit led by our leader of the psychedelic consciousness movement.

"Heavenly blues, by God, by God, heavenly blues by God." Frenzied cult leaders singing away, led by Timothy Leary, with a choir, going full tilt Heavenly Blues. (Think of the wild church scene in 'The Blues Brothers' movie, led by Reverend James Brown.)

Abbie Hoffman, hair tucked in his hat, stepped up to the podium, taking control of the room simply by waving his hand, followed by those eyes scanning the crowd. He spoke almost hypnotically explaining the details of how his program would work. EZ PZ 123 using charts and a pointer as props. Ushers passed out pine cones at the appropriate time, timing is everything with these guys. Man were they good, Butch would've loved this show.

It was like being on the set of "The Rainmaker" watching a master flim flam man, conning the elite of Los Angeles area cult leaders (con artists themselves, many would say) into unknowingly providing free LSD for millions of people.

The who's who of LA cult leaders embraced Abbie Hoffman's Yippie vision, the rest, as they say, is history. There are now hundreds of thousands of miles of roads from Malibu to New York with Heavenly Blue & Pearly Gate Morning Glories waiting to be harvested as free LSD for the people.

What the cult leaders didn't know

They really were helping to plant enough free LSD to get millions of people tripping at the same time.

I was on the back end where the motto is. "Save the bullshit for the fans, not the players."

Cult kids, combined with the military grade triple redundancy standards required by our inner circle of the Youth International Party loosely known as TAP, set up an insurance policy of sorts.

TAP YIPPIE infiltration placed three qualified applicants in all fifty states to apply or get in line to purchase seeds for the State Highway Dept. The number hired was classified, but Frank Discussion remembers hearing thirty-three in hushed tones a few years later.

Jerry Rubin said this was to ensure "Heavenly Blues" are standard issue highway plants thanks to Lady Bird Johnson's "Keep America Beautiful" program.

Most TAP infiltrators are retired at the time of this writing. Thankfully those deep cover Yippie's made sure there is free LSD for the people growing along state highways everywhere in the Land of the Frei.

God Bless the Technical Assistance Program (TAP), arm of the Youth International Party (YIP or YIPPIES).

FREE LSD FOR THE PEOPLE; ENDING WAR FOR GOOD!

After a very successful graveside meeting, I'm sitting in Oppenheimer's idling car contemplating a drive up Chevy Chase to the estate or Monte's resort. Old Bear Strongarm along with a man later identified as the leader of TAP but never named, walked toward me exclaiming, "Wait a minute, he wanted to ask you something." I nodded toward the TAP dude.

The stranger came up to my window, lowering his voice. "Bear said you know Univac at the lab on a personal basis," in a hushed tone.

Looking in the car, his eyes landed on the Doohickey box with the red light, then directly into my eyes, he said, "Here's a shopping list. If you can get even one of those, you are a miracle worker." He stuffed a folded note card into my top pocket.

"Univac at the lab, my ass. Nobody can get in there. It's the tightest security on the planet." Said like he knew everything, when in fact he doesn't know jack shit about our secret hometown game. It's been secret until now that I'm telling my tale.

As Frank Discussion, totally nonplussed, I replied, "Haven't played on that old Sperry in a while. I'll take a look, but no promises."

Coolly putting Oppenheimer's car into gear, I discretely weaved through a crowd of Los Angeles cult dignitary elite, with a wave over my shoulder.

Rolling out I zipped past the gates without slowing at the baby brat bone yard, hooking a right up the Chevy Chase heading to the old Douglas castle in Flintridge.

Playing our Secret Hometown Game

Let's Breach Security at JPL.

They built America's spaceships in my hometown.

Jet Propulsion Laboratory, located in La Canada Flintridge, California, was founded by outlaw scientist Jack Parsons in 1936. Now it's 'Deep Space Control' control center for our little blue planet.

All that spooky secret classified spacecraft, futuristic weapons, alien stuff, marriage of a ginormous Cray supercomputer to a big Sperry Univac 3-story mainframe computer that you might have heard about as conspiracy theory or rumor, standing before me in all its glory.

Whatever you may have heard is disinformation unless it's about the alien technology or mountains packed with old spaceship nuclear reactors that never flew. I'll bet you've never heard about the pi tin in the clean room back in 1975.

It all started by telling Monte Mellman and Bruce Spunkmiester about never getting in trouble for anything I did at the Lab or underground city. Dad used to bring me along a couple, three weekends a month for a few years since I was five or six. We started playing "Let's Breach Security" at age fourteen, almost four years ago, at JPL within walking distance from our respective homes.

One day in 1965 my dad brought me to a meeting, where the great Werner Von Braun was lecturing on telemetry to slingshot off the moon. Dad had taught me about basic telemetry a few months earlier and it was something I was interested in as a 7-year old. As he was talking I blurted out, "But he's wrong, its way off he's going to miss the target." Dad shushed me and you could hear a pin drop in that room.

Chance encounter Werner von Braun

Von Braun announced in his very German, always sounding pissed off voice. "Bring zee child up." Crossing his arms, tapping his foot, is shuffled to the front of the room. We were standing by a chalkboard with a rocket trajectory lined out on it. Herr Direktor handed me his pointer stick and said "Where am I wrong, you show me the science, show me your math." Scowling like a schoolmaster forcing that stick in my hand.

I was ready to shit my pants but for some reason could see the proper formula in my mind. I pointed the pointer stick to a spot on the arc of his chalkboard trajectory, then said. "You are about 2 to 2-1/2 degrees off right here, if you go with that trajectory you will miss the moon and be headed toward Mars, sir." While I paused looking about the room every one of those genius scientists, whomever all had their slide rules out, checking my computations.

Von Braun growled, "Well Mister Burke what makes you think that you are right and I am wrong?" staring into my seven year old incorrigible eyes. I replied "I dunno exactly but it's something about the gravitational weight, mass pull combined with slingshot speed going into the turn, I can just see it."

Just then one of the slide rule dudes spoke up saying, "The kid is right, he's off by 2. Aught degrees and it will miss on that trajectory." Or some scientific rocket scientist talk like that, they all verified what I saw just looking at the old krauts chalkboard listening to him drone.

After that they tested me out with a 167 IQ, then started to treat me special. I was pulled into stuff as a 7-year old boy genius, with zero fucks to give. Except I wanted to impress my dad using what he taught me and what I learned on my own, using my curse, the curse of understanding how things work, seeing the big picture without doing the math.

It was only after getting into mischief on a highly classified government project run by Einstein and Oppenheimer. Something about almost shanking time, whatever that means. I was declared "incorrigible", sending me back from the desert and that wild ride home with Oppenheimer in his fucking car. The teleportation kids program is probably still classified; I'm about to reveal another national secret involving a special pi tin placed on a spacecraft that is still flying with a shitty gold record strapped to its side.

Prior to becoming Frank Discussion, Billy Burke was a boy scout in the JPL troop. I was honored with being unceremoniously kicked out of the teleportation kids program as the only person labeled "incorrigible" by the others for almost shanking time in 1938 walking out a door that was unlocked, looking for candy/adventure, oops. An agent from the project caught me buying pastries in a Swedish bakery as I was about to pay using 1960's American coins. They all said I almost shanked time and everyone was really pissed off at me, but all they did was yell and make me sit in different chairs.

As Frank Discussion, I did everything from stealing their electric cars in the tunnels, ditching classes, skipping into other timelines, dimensions, reprogramming computers, firecrackers, smoke bombs, whatever I could think of that was opportunistic at the moment to raise a little hell or commotion.

Punishment? Before shanking time, all they did was yelling at me or make me learn how to play another musical instrument or some other skill testing. I guessed using the wrong currency for the wrong year was a bit over the top. Maybe I was escaping that contraption to get away from shitty government food. It's not time for that story yet. Wait until Tales from the Underground Cities.

Walt Disney's Grave to Monte's Resort

My entire being was enveloped or cloaked in the persona of Frank Discussion as I drove Oppenheimer's car about two miles, leaving that YIPPIE/cult leader meeting at Walt Disney's grave in Forest Lawn, Glendale to visit Monte's resort, the old Douglas of McDonnell Douglas palatial estate in Flintridge.

Monte had been my best friend since early high school, always up for adventure of any sort. Leaving the boneyard, turning right on Chevy Chase, seventeen minutes later in his turret room of the castle smoking weed smiling a wicked grin looking over a pile of Peyote, Monte said he wanted to meet Mescalito.

Loud live music outside emanating from a rooftop stops abruptly, stilling the room. Monte walks to the window shouting down to the band on his garage roof, "All Along the Watchtower, Hendrix not fucking Dylan." Returning back to me sitting at a table, he got a shit-eating grin. "Mescalito is supposed to make you invisible." A distant look shone in his eyes as a wicked smile crossed his face and the band broke into a familiar tune.

I had an idea to make a challenge. Monte loves a challenge. "Wanna play a serious round of Let's Breach Security tonight, since we are going to be invisible?"

Looking at Monte then alternately at Bruce in my mocking, you're a pussy voice, oozing with insolence, "No I'm on the run from military school, heck, I'm wanted in four states for all I know. How do we know if they have changed anything with security from last time? This is some serious shit, guys. I dunno." Spewing my words, as if these spoiled sons of wealthy families, oozing money were chicken, or worse, they were pussies.

Bruce, a first cousin to the DuPont's parents richer than Monte's, lit a joint of Angel Dust and started laughing. "We had a truck and lab coats last time. They didn't get close."

He laughed, cackling, handing his joint to me who, smelling chemicals, handed that duster back without taking a drag. Bruce was spaced; he didn't even notice I passed on his PCP-laced mint leaves. "Still have clean lab coats bagged in the tack room."

Monte was one of the smartest, most enterprising people I've met in life. He got off on pushing people around him to their limits while relentlessly testing his own; he had none. Truly a limitless individual if there ever was one.

His room was an actual turret in a mansion castle built by an aviation magnate back in the day. Monte produced a large wooden salad bowl filled with what he said was five pounds of dried, plucked, Indian cured, ready to consume, peyote buttons.

We simply needed a ritual first, always a ritual of some sort.

*M*onte lit a package of incense sticks on a small Santeria altar his aunt, a high priestess from Ecuador, had consecrated for him during her last visit, when she blessed our small tight knit group, he then started chanting.

Om yo rah say Coon u sall day

Om you rah say Coon u sall day

Monte Mellman's waving bundled incense made me feel effects of the weed. We started to eat those nasty peyote buttons, washed down with hot tea. Peyote has one of the most unusual flavors of anything in the drug, culinary, or things tasted in life world. By the way, the tea was laced with mescaline unbeknownst to me; I thought it was part of the leftover Chinese food delivery we had been munching on. It was good; I drank almost the whole pot. 40 hits of mescaline as brain lube for those peyote buttons.

The rest of our afternoon was a typical day at what everyone called "Monte's Resort" in that magical castle high atop a hill in Flintridge. Swimming in their pool, a couple three games of pool, enjoying food from leftover Chinese, to almost anything in the always well-stocked Mellman kitchen. Drugs of just about any flavor, type, high, or whatever that one might want abounded. Today it was tea laced with about forty hits of mescaline along with what seemed like twenty or thirty peyote buttons.

You may think you have tripped & tripped hard, that wasn't jack shit compared to this trip, I was holding onto the walls when nothing was happening. Tripping hard but I still was not close to peaking according to Monte it would take some time to be ready for Mescalito.

Sometime after 3:00 AM all three of us, Monte Mellman, Bruce Spunkmiester, Frank Discussion, loaded into a new Mercedes Benz. Driving unnoticed into the Flintridge riding club which abuts the outer JPL complex, into the DuPont's private barn. Monte killed its lights and engine as we rolled through open bar doors, coasting with the clutch pushed into a silent stop.

Bruce jumped out of the still moving car, quietly closing the barn doors. He pulled a hidden key out of its spot, opening a locked door marked Tack Room. Monte and I followed as Bruce moved a saddle then removed a piece of plywood revealing a hidden closet cache.

"Engineer Burke, Doctor Mellman, and Bruce Barf the Janitor," Bruce said, smiling, handing each of us a cleaned, pressed, bagged white lab coat, complete with JPL badges Frank had nicked. I used my Dad's old one with a new date and my picture. There were three pairs of yellow rubber-soled JPL approved dipshit security shoes we silently put on.

Shoes, armed security guards were trained to look for passes with pictures that matched and one of five types of shoes. Who would've thunk it, one of the top-secret security access requirements was a specific type of shoe worn with yellow soles?

Rootie Toot Toot & Yellow Security Soles

Rootie, toot, toot, rootie toot, toot, we are the boys from the institute. Fucking Caltech nerds always thinking up some weird shit to justify gazillions of dollars spent on nerd toys.

I looked at my companions, asking, "Have either of you been here since last summer, any changes in perimeter security? You know how they like to change things up."

Monte started getting a wicked grin lacing up his shoe. "Mescalito makes us invisible, they have caca, mierde, shit for security, they will never catch us."

Lighting a Marlboro, Monte continued with a reminiscing look. "Raymundo and I took a truck last time, we ate breakfast in the cafeteria, caca." Laughing to himself reliving that memory in his peyote infused mind. "Mescalito says we can do anything."

With that he was up the ladder, pushing open a hatch to the roof. We quickly followed him. I popped my head through to witness Monte Mellman running as hard as he could from the peak of this DuPont barn roof.

Monte was screaming, "To Maaaars! Mescalito says fly to Mars, motherfuckers." Pushing off from the roof, flying a good four feet over the top of the barbed wire he shouted, "Aye, yai, yai, why," landing then rolling in a deeply mulched raised bed planter. "Not."

There were poles with electronic housing that shot beams of light out along the interior of the fence line.The planter was a geographic barrier laced with super-secret intrusion technology. Monte literally flew over the nation's tightest perimeter security, powered by the wings of Mescalito.

"Holy shit," I muttered. "I've never seen anyone go in that way before."

Monte was on his feet, pulling his lab coat out of his knapsack. He grabbed a baggie of white powder walking back toward the barn and fence. "Shhh," shushing us, tossing a handful of what turned out to be baseball line chalk into the air toward the fence.

The air lit up with purple, blue, and red laser lines that we all knew were not a hallucination. They had beefed up the perimeter with the blue, we didn't know what it was or did, just 'Don't break any beads of light' and we were cool.

Monte has a look of anticipation motioning to his companions. "Mescalito says it's going to hurt a little when you land but he'll take care of the pain." He carefully throws the rest of the dust. "Hurry up; we don't wanna stay on the fence, do we?"

Standing at the top of the roof I could see my landing spot in that back parking lot. I knew this would be the first time going in without the cover of Dad being a big shot. Thinking Dad, heck, I haven't talked to him in almost two months when I was back at Saint John's Military School in Salina, Kansas.

At that moment the biggest blackest crow with fiery red trinitite eyes lit like Christmas lights dove at me, violently screaming, "Caw, caw, go, go, NOW!"

Needing no further encouragement, I cleared that barbed wire not quite as high as Monte, noticing Bruce was in the air next to me.

We landed, tucked, rolled in unison springing up into a low crouch like a pair o' kung fu fighters. After putting on our lab coats, Bruce tossed his knapsack back over the fence onto the stable roof.

Monte motioned to us, his eyes twinkling. "This way, I learned something new last time," walking like he owned the place toward large ominous lab buildings containing over half of the national secrets on the planet. All we had to do was make it past an inner security gate, then we were in like Flynn.

Monte walked toward an area in the parking lot with a number of golf carts; they all had keys in them. Choosing a sporty looking cart with seats for four, Caltech blue surrey top, tassels hanging down. "Jump in." He expertly put it in gear backing up to us.

We jumped in and Monte drove right through the JPL main gate, smiling and waving at the security guard who barely looked up from his book and waved back at us like we were regular nerds.

"Nothing ever happens here; everyone is afraid of the ghosting stories about those Russian spies last year. Where do you want to go this time?" Monte was gloating driving that cart like a boss, a smirk across his face, eyes a-twinkling.

Pulling out the TAP list from my pocket, I look at it saying, "Yeah, right, I've got to spend some time on Sperry Univac, you know, the Cray building."

Bruce gets a look of disdain on his face. "You and that fucking computer, it's so boring. What can you do with a computer? I want to see the spaceships again. Monte, stop here, meet me in the clean room later." We were passing a massive three-story, city block long and wide building with a small sign: 'Clean room personnel only.'

Monte deftly pulls the golf cart to the VP's parking spot next to the main entrance of this large empty building. "Down the first set of stairs to your left, then right. The clean room fans are a half hour blow. I'll meet you down there in a few."

Drop Off @The Clean Room

Historical note: The Vice President of the United States of America is technically; always the head honcho of NASA something in a nazified charter Werner Von Braun created that was approved by Congress. Go figure number two always being in charge of deep space control center.

Bruce Spunkmeister exits our cart, walking through never locked doors, giving us an OK signal with his fingers quietly slipping in.

We silently drive across an almost deserted JPL campus. A person walking here and there, always in a lab coat, ID badge, wearing approved shoes. Monte drives past a three-square block city mechanical monstrosity reaching three to five stories.

Looking over at me, asking, "I wonder what that is for." He was pointing at a monstrous jumble of pipes and machinery looking like a backdrop for a science fiction movie or something steampunk, mechanically ominous, curiosity seeping from his balls to the walls, tripping harder than hard, being.

I'm focused on getting into Univac again, simply replying, "It's the cooling towers for the computer; hope that thing doesn't fire up while I'm in there. It's a noisy contraption. I've got a list from some YIPPIEs today." Monte pulls the cart around the corner to the front of the building. Continuing I leaned in telling him. "Their top cyber dude thought getting here where we are, takes an act of God or is impossible, I hope that contraption there doesn't fire up, it's loud, really fucking loud, that's why they only run it during the day."

There are signs "Sperry Univac – Cray Center" with the building set in a campus-like setting with park benches, greenery to make the entrance welcoming. Monte pulls up to one of five open spots closest to the doors.

Looking like nerdy scientist types, we walked through the unlocked double glass doors to be greeted by a uniformed security guard sitting at a desk.

Guard barely glanced as I spoke in a semi-animated manner to Monte. "The telemetry computations have to be correct. There is no way Doctor Pickering is right on this. Why the fuck did he have to wake me up to double check his work again?"

Invisibly walking past what is supposed to be the tightest security on the planet, I looked back waiting for the elevator. The guard was sipping coffee out of a white Styrofoam cup, never looking away from his newspaper, reading it, searching for meaning in his well-planned, yet empty life.

We enjoyed an uneventful elevator ride to the third floor control room for the JPL Sperry Univac – Cray Center. This is truly holy ground for people called hackers, actually crackers who like to crack into remote systems. Writing and editing this story, when I get to this part, I am humbled that for some unknown reason, my sandbox as a child prodigy is:

This machine birthed what is now known as the Internet!

She is THE first computer connected to a network of fourteen (count 'em, fourteen) other mainframe computers with black ops funding in the 1960s prior to DARPA and the Gopher Holes, she's wired to 224 mainframe computers this now.

Rows upon rows upon rows of nine-track magnetic tape computing machines, all strung together with wires to communicate. There are two floors below I had only peeked into; because they were filled with humongous computers, tubes, transistors, wires; an old nazified paperclip 'engineering' dude once told me there are over 250,000 miles of thin copper wires on this one machine.

That's enough to reach to the moon, OG, you know, a lotta wire.

Silicon chips hadn't been invented yet, hundreds of thousands of computer boards, hand wired with gold, silver, and exotic alloy wire, wrapped around gold plated pins. Tubes, transistors, rectifiers, mechanical gizmos powered this old school Sperry Univac Mainframe Computer.

The main control operator's workstation has four green and white LED round screens, 3 sets of keyboards and all kinds of switches str8 out of a Hollyfuckingwood Sci-Fi movie. There are radar types of tracking screens on the other side of the room.

Floor to ceiling mainframe big box, gazillion dollar no budget questions, computer components, switches, heating & cooling gauges all kinds of steampunk to 70's state-of-the-art computer gear. I knew how to effortlessly use most all of it. Use it I did, this night of nights Mescalito infused adventure.

Giant four foot tall, six foot long printer stations standing ready in clear acrylic plastic, sound proof, acoustical mufflers like the "Cone of silence" in Get Smart. (Ode to Stan Jolley.)

Muzak is playing "The Girl from Ipanema" over a sound system, piping in gentle sounds throughout the building.

Monte gets a look of pure disgust across his face as if his mind is twisting in pain from Getz – Gilberto. It's elevator music to him. "Where is that muzak puke sack mierde caca music coming from? I've got to do something about that."

Rick [sic] dismafukappears into thin air before my eyes, poof, gone, not even a wisp.

Holy Shit that must be Mescalito, I think as the operator's console begins to float in the room. Nine-tracks are starting to melt visually as the spinning tapes turn on and off, machines start melting into the ground like a cartoon, swirling into government tiled flooring.

"Here, boy, here, boy," calling out like it's a running dog. I'm chasing the operator's booth flying around the room. Quickly and expertly, I jumped like a basketball player grabbing onto the bottom of the chair.

Climbing into the operator's duty chair, putting hallucinations momentarily aside, this adventurer seats up, scanning once very familiar controls, ready to rock for Yippie TAP radicals.

I typed LOGON into the big black keyboard. Moments later a grey screen flickers to life with the word LOGON and a flashing cursor: _. Frank Discussion enters a code they gave me at age seven without thinking it was THE all-access pass given to a seven-year-old for kicks by scientists to see how far a child prodigy could go. They weren't as smart as Oppenheimer who knew I was incorrigible.

Those pompous fucks never changed it because it was the universal master logon. An all-access pass, so to speak. There was no such thing as computer security other than a guard by the door sipping free java in those days.

Univac warms up, the entire room lights up with machines coming to life. A bank of radar screens lights up, spinning radar arms across a grid. Live tracking feeds from remote satellites brighten a bank of video monitors hanging on the opposite wall.

I look around, thinking, "Florida is bullshit. This is deep space control center. I can crash a rocket into Mars if I want, but I don't, that's not cool."

Looking into a TV marked Mariner Live Feed, seeing a crow with glowing red trinitite eyes, flying in darkness of space, red planet behind it.

In my previous life, I had been treated as a prodigy, a boy genius of sorts. Ever since the day in this same room I challenged the calculations of the great Werner Von Braun.

To me, as a seven-year-old, it was a simple calculation on a telemetry curve using the moon's gravity for pull, like a slingshot the old kraut had gotten wrong during a meeting Dad had brought me to; I made the mistake of correcting that old Nazi in front of a group of scientists, oops. Von Braun was wrong, I was right; they treated me "special" after that.

Dad would bring me here after "dentist appointments" or band practice, whatever. It seemed like anytime they had something big, they wanted it checked by "that savant kid" on their $100 million computer system.

It was better than playing the French horn. Damn, how I hated the French horn. They taught me basic COBOL, FORTRAN, along with how to think binary, or maybe I taught them that. Whatever.

Regardless this machine has been my part time toy about ten years.

I'm thinking, Shit, I'm tripping balls. What do those YIPPIEs want again? Pulling that folded index card from my pocket, trying to absorb this unusual TAP request for information.

1. **Dial up computer numbers for all government contractors making nuclear missiles & bombs**

2. **National & International telephone long distance billing codes:**

3. **Atomic bomb prime contractors above**

4. **Military black ops untraceable deep cover phone billing algorithm code generator.**

5. **3. Location of J. Edgar Hoover's dress collection**

I'm flabbergasted thinking out loud. "What the fuck is this, how do I...?" My hands play the command line driven COBOL / F0RTRAN system like a Stradivarius. Trancelike typing into the main console:

Command/list/dod/prime/sic3499.9986/nuke/tel/prom/pt/wats/access keycodes/=connection? syntax+connect&?=disp

Pressing home key, pyramid (now F4) and enter key at the same time.

At that moment background MUZAK changes to Jimi Hendrix "All Along the Watchtower" with a significant increase in the volume. I think, Monte, that motherfucker found the sound box. Mescalito must've brought him there.

Four Banks of nine-track mind ray computing machines light up, spinning huge reels of tape. Another wall of TV monitors lights up. A mechanical computer voice says, "Twelve Prime" as the operator's screen has a green and white display. Twelve Monitors light up, each with the name of a different defense contractor, area code, phone number, computer name, administrator password. Martin Marietta, Lockheed, a dozen household name companies, who delivered death for dear old Uncle Sam.

I look at the screen exclaiming out loud, "Fucking YIPPIEs, how did they know?"

Giving the print command, a printer jumps to life making lots of mechanical noises inside its cone of silence contraption. (Acoustical muffler or very noisey printer silencer.)

Entering a new string of commands, the Univac once again starts the tape devices, not a few but all of them. A temperature gauge on the operator's station begins to rise from green to orange. Shit, what I do now? I'm thinking fuck we don't want to overheat.

Silence as all noises stop, lights dim, tapes stop swirling, just a green screen with white flashing type:

Direct dial billing numbers.

With a list of the who's who of DOD contractors and a string of numbers next to each name. There were about thirty of them, just enough to print on one sheet of paper.

Mind wandering infused by Mescalito, as I watched a Rose Bowl sized space craft descending for landing through the windows of the Sperry Univac control room thinking, "I'm tripping balls. This is not really happening to me, tripping balls I'm on the beach at the Rincon with Oppenheimer's car." The thought of Oppenheimer's car, being Frank Discussion, I realized once again, this is my reality.

I'm at The Lab. Jack Parsons Lab, JP fucking eL.

*O*nce again, I give print command lighting up that noisy big printer under its acoustical covering. This time it only prints one page then goes silent.

Looking at that TAP index card again, reading 'J. Edgar Hoover's dress collection', yeah, right this must be a prank from Abbie Hoffman. OK, let's see what we get, but how do I query this?

After trying a number of commands, which led nowhere, I thought, what Hoover, as in J. Edgar, mister big of the G men. Dresses, thinking:

J. Edgar Hoover collects dresses, maybe, like I collected girls' bicycle seats in my sophomore year of high school? Those are still hanging on our garage wall in La Cañada, like trophies in my boyish man cave.

Hitting one more command query, our deep space computer control room lit up like a pinball machine. The entire bank of TV monitors that had previously been listing nuclear bomb makers each showed three letters – FBI.

Oh shit, oh shit. Holy fucking shit is the only thing going through my mind. I looked out the window, noticing two cars pulling up quickly in the parking space Monte had used earlier.

Pressing the exit command, everything dies down. I bolt from the command center seat making a beeline to the printer. Grabbing the papers, folding them unconsciously, slipping papers into my shirt, quickly exiting the door. Hearing voices on the steps I hit the elevator button, the door opens, get in pressing floor 1, breathing a sigh of relief.

The elevator goes down with Cream playing "Sunshine of your love" on the MUZAK piped into the elevator.

Elevator doors slid open to an empty hallway, a view of one of the cars pulling away, and guard with his back to me, still searching that newspaper for meaning in his empty life. Being Frank Discussion, cool as a cucumber, I walk by that guard who grunts, "Shift change?" without looking up from his paper. I light up a Phillip Morris Commander after exiting the building to enjoy during my short two block walk to the clean room building.

JPL campus alone in the wee hours of the morning is truly a unique experience.

*T*hinking makes things happen here. I was starting to think of something profound, then – WHOOSH – a crow with glowing red eyes flew out of nowhere toward my head. I just hit that commander, looked it in the eyes, then smiled, exhaling a smoke ring that grew larger, then larger, engulfing the crow as it rose skyward toward the stars.

My thoughts drifted, wondering what type of black magic Parsons was using with Einstein. Why did the old Nazi tell me, "Your space program is founded on black magic from the ancient ones"? Every time he was drunk at the house or underground city, it was black magic rocketry, Schnapps & lederhosen dancers playing accordions stories.

Thought leadership my ass.

Those old paperclip Nazis were a trip, always something out of left field with them.

———————◆———————

A mystical pentagram made of pure light rose out of nowhere. I looked close. It was made of light that kept getting whiter and brighter each millisecond. Red glowing, trinitite eyes of that crow appeared at the center of this mystical object in the heart of deep space control center.

Without flapping a wing, Bre'r crow flew what seemed like light speed through this laser bright pentagram, eyes locked on me. "Caw, cawed." This time I ducked. Damn thing almost hit me. I watched a moment then back to a psychedelic light show turning hard, deep, purple. Proof – gone.

I could hear Cream playing over the PA system, taking another drag off my Commander while walking briskly toward my last stop of this adventure.

Psst, It's a National Secret

I approached the north end of the clean room building; the place we dropped Bruce off at is the center or main entrance. Dipping into this stairway as I had so many times before, seeing a number pad, entering #4386*, hearing a hard buzzing electrical click, pulling the door open.

The door opens into a side entrance of America's premier satellite payload manufacturing facility. They operate twenty-four hours a day technically, but it's a Caltech 8:30 AM until 3:30 PM gravy job. Around the clock bullshit is for when the VP is in town or a high profile something going on with the global media.

JPL is infamous for its founder, Jack Parsons, the father of American rocketry, Order of Thelema (OTO) and resurrecting a long dead flavor of sexual magic after starting his lab in a nearby Arroyo Seco ditch.

It's rumored that Jack Parsons' death was a hoax

*H*e *really rode the throne of EL through an inter-dimensional tear on hot Santa Ana winds. Jack still pops up every now and again riding that chair contraption of his, stuck between life & death. Yet another unrelated, related story or adventure, perhaps told another now to those with an ear to hear.*

JPL is more famous for building the first American satellite to be launched into orbit, Explorer 1 in 1957, sparking a space race between the good Americans vs. the bad Russian Soviet Bear. It was built just forty-three feet from where I'm standing, wondering why it smelled like someone was smoking weed in the building.

I don't know if the specifics of the JPL clean room are even classified. It's kind of like in the movie Independence Day where they are at Area 51 (kind of but not quite) going down a hallway with clean room gear at the top.

Different stops blow air and/or mist chemicals on a suited person to ensure the spacecraft is never contaminated by "ordinary items" from Earth. Raised grated floors, standing in front of misting nozzles, dryers in general a pain in the ass.

After all a few blankets "innocently" given to Native Americans wiped out entire civilizations from diseases they had no immunity to.

All the far-out Star Trek hockie pockey Imagineering that modern science fiction is made from surrounding these impudent infiltrators seeking adventure.

I look at the rack of suits, they are all there thinking I don't want to suit up and go down there. I'm done, ready to go. Everybody has to be geek suited up for clean room entry; it takes time and is of suck.

Suddenly lower glass doors open revealing Monte driving a golf cart right up the ramp. Automatic doors open before him; he pulls up as the top doors automatically open, slides a few donuts on the slick concrete outside the top entrance. Monty is just laughing, smoking a huge joint sporting an open can of beer in the cup holder of the golf cart. He slides up to me, Cheshire grin, arm outstretched handing off a fresh beer saying, "Get in, you have to see this."

I flop into the back seat cracking open that ice cold beer, absconded from a clean room workers' fridge. Monte punches it back down the ramp, flicking a strong, burning 'hot boxed' joint at the wall then spitting a humongous [sic] loogie passing through lower doors. I'm thinking if they ever find out about this, it's going to take months to decontaminate the facility.

Monte drives like a frenzied mad man being chased by a bat out of hell down a big hallway to flashing red lights with black and yellow signs reading: AUTHORIZED PERSONNEL ONLY. Without slowing down, he drives through a pair of swinging doors with big rubber bumpers, does a doughnut on the slick concrete, stopping with a shit-eating grin on his face, with a perfect P.T. Barnum / Vanna White arm.

Voyager and the Pi tin

*T*here *it is in all its glory, Voyager, complete with gold record strapped to its side. Just like everything I had read about it, years in the making, a masterpiece.*

This room is a holy of holies to space geeks and science fiction nerds.

I'd seen it through the glass many times, but only inside once on a previous clandestine mission with Monte & Raymundo on a dare. This is where they built our planet's fleet of spacecraft.

The real deal, not like those prop houses off Lankershiem, these things are made to fly thousands of years. Engineered tighter than a Bentley, that's saying something.

The closer I got to this spectacular spacecraft, the more it smelled like shit. I mean poop, caca, feces, a turd. It smelt like the bathroom at

Mijares after $3.99 all you can eat lunch. It smelled like someone took a honking dump in the cleanest clean room on the planet.

"Ha haha caca haha caca." Bruce Spunkmiester has a stupid PCP, peyote and who knows what else induced laugh. He runs up to me wearing his street clothes with a pi tin in his hand that has a huge steaming turd in it.

Poop in a Pi Tin

"Poop in a pi tin, you are a sick fuck. Get that out of here, it stinks like shit," Frank Discussion's response while backing away, knocking over some expensive piece of lab equipment with a crash.

Bruce waves his prized poop under my nose. Jumping back as I tried to knock it out of his hand, he said, "I have an idea."Climbing into a cherry picker that is set up to work on the spacecraft, he carefully placed his precious pi tin on its tool holder tray, pushing the joystick, bumpy at first, going up, then in, easing that contraption into place.

Bruce Spunkmiester reaches up atop the Voyager, holding his poop in a pi tin, beaming as if he had just climbed Mount Everest. Taking a pen from his pocket protector, he dips it in pooh then writes something on that gold record in human feces.

Monte lets out a wicked Mescalito fueled burst of laughter ending with, "Mierde, caca, that's really gross, you are one sick individual. Let's get out of here."

"I hereby christen thee Voyager. Fare thee well." Bruce Spunkmiester places his poop in a pi tin in a prominent position on the spacecraft where (as if it wouldn't be) it would be easily noticed.

He expertly navigates that cherry picker back down to the floor saying, "I wish I had a camera. Nobody is ever going to know it's DuPont crap on…"

I shook my head in disgust at what I'd just witnessed. "It's going to take months to decontaminate. Guys, we promised to never destroy anything."

Monte snorted. "Nothing's destroyed; nothing is contaminated, just a little stinky pooh for that golden record." He looked at his watch. "Seventeen minutes until the first bus of the day. Let's go. You know the drill."

We all knew that meant time to hit the bricks, riding out the side doors up to the cafeteria, Monte parked the buggy, grabbed a free cup of coffee, and then casually walked to the waiting RTD bus. The driver looked at us. "Long nights, last run. Take a seat, gentlemen, we are about to roll."

The big RTD bus drove those seditious, security breaching teenagers through the gates; we jumped out at the first stop, Flintridge Riding Stables, sans lab coats.

Now you know the secret of America's most highly secure clean room being defaced with defecation on an exploratory space vehicle. Poop in a pi tin from a DuPont's stinky butt hole is still traveling the universe. If they only knew that when they made the Star Trek movie about this very same spacecraft years later, it might have had a different twist.

Needless to say this adventure, as with many others, never made the press. We were never caught. Frank Discussion is the only one left living and has zero fucks to give about telling this story.

It's a very shitty national secret that even workers at the lab thought was urban legend, until I told a few after drunkenly beating the JPL badminton champ left handed in Altadena a few years ago. Oops, you should've seen the looks on their faces as I told this story aloud for the first time ever.

Yeah, that really happened. What can I say?

*B*adboy, Badboy, whatcha gonna do when they come *for you?*

Bruce Spunkmiester and Monte Mellman are both safely entombed at Forest Lawn Hollywood.

They no longer care if I tell this crappy story.

What can I say, it wasn't me doing the stinky pooh, T'was Bruce.

What can I say?

The end book one I Stole Oppenheimer's Car.

Go to  www.istoleoppenheimerscar.com

For the special online deals.

Coming Attractions from Billy Burke

D iscover what Doctor Oppenheimer has planned for incorrigible frank discussion.

Book Two

Tales from The Underground Cities, Part 1.

Book Three

A Trip to Bohemian Grove as Honored Guests in Oppenheimer's Car.

Special online details at

www.istoleoppenheimerscar.com

Book Two

Tales from The Underground Cities, Part 1.

Free Sample Chapter 1

Atomic Clouds over Queen Mod Land

*A*s Frank Discussion, I woke up alone, enjoying an unusual heat wave New Year's Day, 1976 at La Conchita. One of the garage doors was open toward the ocean. The window let in a slight breeze. Just a do-nothing kind of day. Oppenheimer's car was parked in its spot back of the lot. My only visitor was a crow.

I was lying on the couch smoking cigarettes, watching Captain Kangaroo on the black and white TV connected to rabbit ear antenna. Looking at the stash jar, thinking the weed is getting low – only about a quarter pound remaining. Going to have to do something about that. A pair of finches landed on the fencepost in my line of sight while Mister Green Jeans was doing his routine.

I got up and walked out the doors; the finches flew to a higher perch on the roof. I noticed a TV news camera van on the north end of the beach just below the point. Hmmm, "That's the other channel," I said out loud walking back to change the channel.

An older, white-haired national new anchorman appeared on the snow channel with an atomic 'Oppenheimer' mushroom cloud pictured behind him. "…that's it – we have several unconfirmed reports of multiple nuclear explosions over Antarctica approximately fifteen minutes ago, reported from Queen Mod Land; now back to your regularly scheduled programming."

The television image went to a shot of a reporter with his back to the ocean, saying "So far thirty-three large bales of marijuana have washed ashore, presumably from an offshore smuggler dumping the contraband to avoid capture…" I bolted back to the door, then without thinking took off on foot down the hill toward the dog tunnel leading under Pacific Coast Highway.

The Rincon is a place where most people traveling North or South on Pacific Coast Highway don't notice a sleepy little seaside village nestled in the foothills.

Rincon is a short beach that ends at the highway built up with giant boulders. Pacific surf laps below the U.S. 101 at high tide. In front of La Conchita, their beach extends twenty to one hundred feet from the highway, but it's hard to get to, very hard, cars flying by at highway speeds with a wall on the seaside of the highway.

The north end is Rincon Point, best winter surfing in the golden state (Ventura/Santa Barbara County Line). One can ride a swell a quarter to a half mile like out of a dream, but it's pretty much locals only, unless you're eLitE. The other side of those mountains is filled with oil fields pumping black gold, and avocados for the Getty family every day.

The edge of Pacific Coast Highway below the embankment there are drainage tunnels about five feet tall Pez dispenser shaped opening, about twenty feet wide made from concrete and steel after WWII. Dog tunnels run under the highway. It's the way most locals bring their dogs on wagons filled with beer and firewood to their semi-private beach.

I made my way through the dog tunnel hunched over like Quasimodo, emerging on a sandy beach. My eyes went directly to several bales wrapped in black industrial plastic washing up to the beach, gently bobbing in the surf's foam. Quickly scanning the surf to see a dozen or so more bales O' weed bobbing in the surf, carefully measuring distances in my mind's eye.

Immediately I ran to the nearest one, never taking my eyes off of it. I pulled that heavy bale out of the water with Popeye strength, as if I had blinders on, only seeing free weed. I started lugging my prize back toward the tunnel. Bam! Out of nowhere a big fat (think Jackie Gleason) fully uniformed Ventura County Sheriff sergeant wearing aviator glasses was standing there grinning at me.

Hearken the gryphon; from darkness into light, illuminated with Babylon's illusion.

I can remember that man's grin to this day like he was the cat that ate the canary, whom slowly in a purposeful drawl said, "If I was you, I'd just drop that bale right there and walk on like I never saw you, geet-chee-yaw boy. Walk away now, that's right, walk on home to Momma, boy."

Made in the USA
Columbia, SC
08 August 2023

21165583R00070